the
LAST
CHANCE
TEXACO

brent hartinger

the LAST CHANCE TEXACO

HARPERTEMPEST
An Imprint of HarperCollins*Publishers*

Y

The Last Chance Texaco

Copyright © 2004 by Brent Hartinger

www.harpertempest.com

Library of Congress Cataloging-in-Publication Data
Hartinger, Brent.

The last chance Texaco / by Brent Hartinger.

p. cm.

Summary: Troubled teen Lucy Pitt struggles to fit in as a new tenant at a last-chance foster home.

ISBN 0-06-050912-0 — ISBN 0-06-050913-9 (lib. bdg.)

[1. Foster home care—Fiction. 2. Orphans—Fiction.]

I. Title.

PZ7.H2635Las 2004	2002152945
[Fic]—dc21	CIP
	AC

Typography by Hilary Zarycky

1 2 3 4 5 6 7 8 9 10

First Edition

For Michael Jensen,
the person I call home

And for Jennifer DeChiara,
who will always be welcome to visit

the
LAST
CHANCE
TEXACO

1

The door was locked, and I sure as hell didn't have the key.

I was standing on a front porch, and the door before me was tall and wide and arched, with a fancy black iron handle and hinges, like the door to a church or a haunted house. I should know—I'd been dragged into a whole lot of different churches over the years, and while none of the many houses I'd lived in had actually been haunted, most of them had been plenty scary.

But this wasn't the door to a church or a house like any I'd been in before. No, it was the entrance to this big mother of a mansion looking out over the bay. Years ago, back when this place was the home of Mr. Rich Bastard, Esquire, and his wife, Greedula, the house had probably even had a name. I'm-So-Impressed Manor, or something like that.

But that had been a long time ago, and the door had taken its share of scratches and scuffs since then. The rest of the house had pretty much gone to the dogs too, with peeling paint and crooked gutters and a shaggy yard where all the plants seemed to be overgrown and dying at exactly the same time. So now the place had a different name. Kindle Home. It had a different purpose too, about as far as you could get from the one it had been built for, which was to house filthy-rich people and impress the neighbors. Now it was a group home for teenagers in "state custodial care." Orphans and shit. It also happened to be my new home.

Why am I spending so much time describing this house and its damn front door? Because this is partly the story of that house, and I figured I should start at the very beginning. And unless you break in through a window, which I've been known to do, you first enter a house through its front door. Which, as I've already told you, in this case was locked.

"It's not locked," Leon said. "Sometimes you just need to give it a good kick."

Leon was the guy standing behind me on the front porch. He was the Kindle Home counselor who'd picked me up at my former group home that morning to bring me here. He was a little like the house itself, because he hadn't been what I was expecting at all. For one thing, he was Native American. "Lucy Pitt?" he'd said to me thirty minutes earlier, in the front room of my old group home. "I'm Leon Dogman." In group homes, the best way to tell the difference between the kids and the counselors is usually the color of their skin, and just for the record, it's not the counselors who are black and brown and red. Leon was also younger than most counselors, probably still in his twenties, and he had a scraggly black beard and a pierced eyebrow and three visible tattoos.

But even if Leon didn't look like the other group home counselors I'd seen, I knew he'd act just like them. I'd been in the foster care system since I was seven years old—a grand total of eight years—and I knew how the adults operated. The first few times I'd screwed up, back when I was seven or eight years old, everyone had said I'd just been upset over the death of my parents. But I was fifteen now, past the Point of No Return, and no counselor or therapist or foster parent had the time or energy to spend on a lost cause like me.

Leon had said to give that front door a kick, so I

gave it a swift one, and what do you know, it opened. Being in foster care as long as I had, I guess I'd learned a lot about swift kicks.

"What'd I tell you?" Leon said. "That's the thing about a big old house like this. Everything is one-of-a-kind. When something breaks, you can't just run over to the hardware store and replace it. So you learn to live with things the way they are." He grinned a little and kind of rolled his eyes. "There's hardly anything in Kindle Home that isn't broken somehow."

I nodded once, trying hard not to look too interested, and pushed my way inside.

I found myself in a front room that led off into other rooms—a foyer, I guess they're called. Directly in front of us was this giant carved stairway that flowed down from a landing halfway to the second floor like a great river of wood.

Leon was still right behind me. "Well, this is it," he said. "Welcome to Kindle Home." He didn't overdo it with the phony enthusiasm, which I appreciated.

I glanced around. There were holes in the walls and burns in the carpet, and the smell of Pine-Sol and burned popcorn in the air. What the hell is it about group homes and burned popcorn? But that staircase was pretty cool. And there was this explosion of a chandelier hanging from the ceiling way over our heads. A few of the bulbs were burned out and it was dusty, but the crystal jingly things still sort of sparkled, and I don't think I'd been that close to anything like it in my life.

"Come on, I'll show you around," Leon said. He looked over at my backpack. "You wanna set that down for a second? We won't go far."

"No," I said. It was heavy, but when everything you own fits into one bag, you learn to keep a pretty good grip on it.

I followed Leon across the foyer. "That was the library," he said, pointing to the door to the right of the front door. "Now it's the office and therapist's room. And there's the kitchen." He gestured to the open doorway to the right of the staircase, and I caught a glimpse of beige linoleum and stainless steel.

Finally, we came to the double doorway to the left of the stairway. It led into an enormous living room that connected to a dining room almost as big, and that, in turn, must have connected back up with the kitchen. The style of furnishing was Classic Group Home: sagging thrift-store sofas, no sharp edges or anything breakable anywhere, and absolutely nothing that anyone could possibly turn into a weapon. It was as close as you could get to a padded cell and still have chairs. But at the same time, there were reminders of the days before the house had become a dumping ground for teenage rejects. Faded gold velvet curtains. A fireplace with a carved wooden mantel that matched the stairway and was almost tall enough to stand upright in. And big sweeping picture windows, which must have once looked down on the water before trees had grown up to block the view.

"Well?" Leon said. "How do you like your new home?" New home? Was he trying to be funny? "Brief rest stop" was more like it. But Leon didn't look like he was being sarcastic. No, his face looked open—warm, even. Either he was a moron or he hadn't read my file yet.

A cat stepped out from behind the couch. He must have been sleeping on the heating duct, because he stretched like he'd just woken up. He was really skinny, with brown tiger stripes, and was pretty mangy too. He was missing a lot of fur, but it was all on the lower half of his body, like he'd licked it off himself. I wasn't surprised. Group home cats were usually just as messed up as the kids.

"That's Oliver," Leon said. "You know, Oliver Twist?"

I looked at him blankly, even though I knew that Oliver Twist was a famous orphan from a book. No need to let Leon know I wasn't a moron.

"Where is everyone?" I asked.

"Upstairs," Leon said. "And I think Ben took some kids to the park."

I nodded, and we both fell silent, watching Oliver saunter out toward the kitchen. I knew that Leon probably wanted me to ask him about the house, that he had what he thought was some great story to tell. But I also knew that if I waited until a few weeks later to start acting chummy, he'd be much more grateful, and I'd get a lot more out of him.

"There's an interesting story about this house," Leon said.

I had to fight to keep from rolling my eyes. Counselors were so incredibly easy to read. But at the same time, I decided to throw this one a bone. "Yeah?" I said.

"It was built by a man named Howard Kindle back in the nineteen-thirties. He was this big timber baron, really rich and really ruthless. But when he died in the nineteen-sixties, he left a will that gave this house to our program, saying we should use it for kids with no homes. As far as we know, he'd never talked to anyone from the program, and he'd never given much money to charity either, so no one could figure out why he'd done what he did. Then, a year after Kindle died, one of our workers was clearing the last of his junk out of the basement, and he made a very interesting discovery."

That he'd been an orphan himself, I thought to myself. Give me a break. This was the oldest story in the book.

"Turns out he'd been murdering people and burying them in the crawl space," Leon said.

"What?" I said. "You're kidding!"

Leon grinned, all teeth and whiskers and dimples. "Yeah. Just wanna see if you're paying attention. Actually, no one knows why he gave his house to us. But boy, his kids sure were pissed. They still live around here, and every couple of years, they try to reopen the case and fight that will all over again. Fact is, I don't care why Kindle did it. I'm just glad he did. There's no other group home like it in the state."

Leon was right about Kindle Home looking different from Bradley Home and Ryden Home and Haply House and the other three group homes I'd lived in. And I hope it goes without saying that none of the four foster families I'd lived with had lived in anything like a mansion, even a run-down, child-proofed mansion like this one. It felt different too. Solid. You could feel it under your feet. The doors stuck, and things might be cracked and dusty, but the underlying structure was sound.

But even if it looked and felt different from the other houses I'd lived in over the years, I knew it wasn't really. Leon hadn't told me the real story behind Kindle Home, the one that mattered to me. He hadn't needed to. Every kid in my foster care district already knew it. To us, Kindle Home was known as the Last Chance Texaco. The name came from those gas stations on long stretches of empty highway, the ones that have signs that say they're the "last chance" to get gas or have repair work for a whole bunch of miles, like right before a big, barren desert.

Kindle Home became a group home in the 1960s. And from the start, it was the group home for the kids who'd screwed up again and again, but who supposedly still had one last shot to turn things around. It wasn't a big, barren desert that came after our Last Chance Texaco—it was a high-security facility for teenagers called Eat-Their-Young Island, the place for the foster care system's truly hopeless cases.

Eat-Their-Young Island was located on a real island, but that wasn't its real name. It was really called Rabbit Island, but some kid had renamed it too, I guess because rabbits sometimes eat their young. Basically, it was a prison for kids. Surveillance cameras. Locks on all the doors, and sometimes restraints on the beds at night. Therapists and counselors could call Rabbit Island a "treatment center" all they wanted, but no one ever got better from their "treatment," and the only way anyone ever got out was by turning eighteen.

I knew I'd be there soon enough. It had taken me eight long years to work my way through The System, but now here I was, at the head of the line. It was only a matter of time before it was my turn to take the ride, only it wasn't a roller coaster we were talking about—not the fun kind, anyway. The counselors here all knew it too, or they would soon enough, once they'd read my file. Their job was to keep me waiting in line until it was my time to ride the Rabbit Island roller coaster.

Standing in the doorway to the living room at Kindle Home, Leon was still looking at me, waiting for me to react to his little story about Howard Kindle.

But I just turned toward the stairway and said, as flatly as I could, "Can I see my room now?" I was tired of talking. Besides, my backpack was heavy and cutting into my shoulders.

"Sure," Leon said. "Follow me upstairs." He didn't sound annoyed at all by my slight, which irritated me more than I wanted to admit.

As we stepped to the base of the stairs, he looked over at my backpack again. "You know," he said, "that thing looks heavy. Any chance you'll let me carry it upstairs?"

2

We caught my new roommate red-handed, with a lit match in her hand.

"Yolanda!" Leon said. "What'd we tell you about smoking inside the house?" He'd knocked on the bedroom door, then opened it, only to find my future roommate just lighting up a cigarette.

At first she tensed, all set to try to throw the cigarette out the window. But when she saw she was busted, she relaxed a little and actually took a drag. "You said I couldn't smoke in the *bathroom*."

Leon rolled his eyes. "Yolanda, don't play that game. You know the rules. That's five points." He glanced out at the hallway and lowered his voice. "Next time . . ."

She ground the cigarette out on the windowsill.

"Lucy," Leon said, "this is your roommate, Yolanda." She was small and pretty, and her skin was the color of the wood in the staircase in the foyer. I had no control over what Leon and the other counselors thought of me, but Yolanda was my roommate. I *could* control what she thought of me, and I knew how important it was to get and stay on her good side.

"Hey," I said.

"Hey," she said, and I couldn't help imagining how I looked through her eyes. White skin, black hair, dark eyes. But even more important than what she could see was what she couldn't see, which was basically anything on my face, anything that I was thinking. The front door of my face was locked and deadbolted, and that was exactly the way I wanted it.

"Well," Leon said to me, "I'll let you get unpacked. Mrs. Morgan will go over the house rules with you tomorrow. Till then, just shout if you have any questions. Bathroom's two doors down."

Then Leon was gone, and I was alone with Yolanda. I closed the door behind him. I used to feel nervous or excited when I first met a roommate, but I wasn't nervous or excited now. How could I be? Meeting a roommate was such a familiar action, something I just had to do every so often, like clipping my toenails.

"That's your dresser," Yolanda said, nodding to one of the chests of drawers and sucking on the unlit cigarette, which I now saw she'd been careful not to bend.

I glanced at the dresser—vintage Goodwill—but I wasn't about to unpack my stuff. Why bother? I knew I wouldn't be here long enough to make it worth my while.

"Where you from?" Yolanda asked, settling back on her bed, watching me. Kids in group homes don't have hometowns or nationalities. They have their previous group home. No matter how many different ones you've lived in, it's only the one right before that matters.

"Bradley Home," I said. "You?"

"Ryden," she said. I'd lived in Ryden for eight months two years earlier, but I didn't tell Yolanda that.

"Like it here?" I said. There was no point in reminiscing about Ryden Home, but talking about the here and now made a lot of sense. Yolanda might tell me something I'd need to know.

"'Sokay," she said. She stared out the window for a second, then said, "My parents were killed in a propane explosion. We were gonna have a barbecue."

Where had that come from? And why was she was telling me this now? This wasn't how things worked. Didn't she know I could someday use it against her?

"How long you been in?" I asked. I meant how long had she been in the foster care system, but I knew she knew that.

"Seven months." Her parents had been killed only seven months earlier? That meant she was a newbie. But seven months and she was already at the Last Chance Texaco? What had she done to end up here so soon? It had to be something worse than smoking inside.

"How 'bout you?" she said.

"Since I was seven," I said. "Eight years." I didn't really remember life before The System, before my parents had been killed in the car accident. There were images in my head, frozen pictures, but they weren't connected to me. They were like snapshots blowing down the sidewalk, farther and farther away from me.

"So you meet Ken and Barbie?" Yolanda asked.

"Shhh," I said.

"What?"

I wasn't exactly sure what. I just knew someone was listening in on us. You live with groups of people long enough, you pick up sort of a sixth sense.

I jerked open the door. Sure enough, there was a kid standing just outside, head bent, like he'd been listening in. He was young, twelve or thirteen, with glasses and a part in the middle of his hair. He had an MP3 player and was wearing the headphones, but I figured he wasn't listening to music. He'd been listening to Yolanda and me through the door. I knew this for sure when he looked up and I saw the shocked expression on his face.

"Hear anything interesting?" I said.

He stood there stunned for a second more. Then he said, "Huh?" He was talking loudly, pretending like he couldn't hear me over the sound of his music.

It was a pretty good recovery, but I knew he was faking. "Give it up," I said. I pointed down to the MP3 player. "The damn thing's not even on."

Once again, I'd left him speechless.

"I'm Lucy," I said to the boy, because I figured why make enemies unless I had to.

"Yeah, I know," he said, trying to sound mysterious, which is hard when you have pimples and a paper clip holding your glasses together.

"That's Damon," Yolanda said.

"Yeah, I know," I said, imitating the mysterious

tone he'd used on me. That got a smile out of him. At least he was smart enough to get my jokes.

"He's a weasel," Yolanda said.

"I know that too," I said. This was mostly bluster, but the fact is, I did know something about him. After a few group homes, you start to see patterns in the kids who live in them. Roles people play, like parts in a movie. I knew immediately what part Damon played. He was the Mole, the guy everyone went to for information about everyone else. Kids in group homes did a lot of trading, and what Damon traded was information.

"Well, Damon," I said, "it's nice to meet you."

"It's not like I—" he started to say, but I shut the door in his face. Yolanda actually squealed in pleasure.

When she'd calmed down a little, she said, "Damon's harmless," but I'd already known that too. That's why I'd closed the door in his face.

It had been a long morning, and I needed to pee, so I waited a second for Damon to make himself scarce—I knew he'd leave after getting busted once. Then I opened the door and headed for where Leon had said the bathroom was.

The bathroom door was locked. Or was it just

stuck? The doorknob turned okay.

I knocked. "Hello?" I said, but there wasn't any answer from inside. What the hell was it about this house and sticky doors?

I was just about to give it a good kick when a voice said, "Occupied."

The voice hadn't come from inside the bathroom, but from farther down the hall.

I turned. There was a girl walking toward me, about my age. Big hair, big boobs, lots-o'-makeup. But there was fire behind that mascara, and I knew it.

"You're new," she said. "I'm Joy." I don't think I'd ever heard anybody sound quite that aloof. I knew immediately that, unlike Yolanda and Damon, this one was trouble. Without thinking, I stepped back from the bathroom.

"Lucy," I said. "There someone in there?" I nodded to the bathroom.

"Not yet," Joy said. She stepped between me and the door, and gave it a good shove with her shoulder. The door squeaked open, and she stepped inside. "But there is now." Then she slammed the door in my face.

Ever wonder where the term "pecking order" comes from? It comes from flocks of chickens.

Chickens create this sort of social ranking where every chicken can peck on any other chicken lower down in the pecking order. The chicken at the bottom of the pecking order is usually the weakest one. And if that chicken's weakness is really obvious—like if it's badly injured—the rest of the flock might even peck it to death.

Just so you know, that's pretty much how it works in group homes too.

Dinner in a group home is the one time when everyone is together in one place. The counselors always say this like it's a good thing. The truth is, dinnertime at a group home is like dusk on the African savannah—it's when everything happens.

That night, Leon called us down to dinner, and I joined Yolanda and Damon at the long table in the big dining room. Leon was in the kitchen cooking with one of the counselors I hadn't met yet.

A second later, Joy breezed into the dining room with another girl, who I'd later learn was named Melanie. Her hair was a little smaller than Joy's, and her makeup was a little thicker. And she was just this side of plump, but the fat was in all the wrong places.

"You're in my chair," Joy said to me.

Yolanda looked up. "We don't have chairs." My roommate may have been in The System for seven months, but it sounded like she hadn't picked up much except smoking. She still didn't know a challenge when she heard one.

"We do so have chairs," Joy said, like it was the most obvious thing in the world. "Don't we, Damon?"

Damon was suddenly fascinated by his spoon. "Oh, yeah." So I'd been right about Damon—at least *he* was smart.

"Fine," I said. I was new here, no reason to make waves. So I stood up and took a seat a chair away from Joy—far enough that I wouldn't have to deal with her all through dinner, but not so far that it looked like I was scared of her.

"Now you're in *my* chair," Melanie said.

Of course I was, I said to myself. I wondered, How many times have they played out this little routine?

Not making waves was one thing, but there was no point in letting myself be pushed around. "Tell you what," I said. "Why don't we share? I'll sit here now, and you can have it after dinner."

That hit Melanie right between the eyes. She was

just about to say something in response when the counselor I hadn't met yet entered with a pitcher of milk from the kitchen. "You must be Lucy!" she said to me. "I'm Gina." She was tall and willowy, with long sandy blond hair.

"Hey," I said, already irritated by all her teeth.

"Hope you like lasagna," she said. I *would* like lasagna, I wanted to say, except I'm allergic to cheese. This was the one part of my file the counselors obviously hadn't read yet. But Gina had disappeared back into the kitchen before I could say anything. It's not like I wanted my three hundred thousandth peanut butter and jelly sandwich, anyway.

When I looked back at Melanie, she'd taken the seat on the other side of Joy, pretending like our little incident with the chairs had never even happened. So I'd won the first round.

Just then, the front door burst open, like someone had had to give it the boot again. A second later, a voice called out, "Hi, honey, I'm home!" and I heard a couple of kids groaning from the foyer. Joy and Melanie groaned too, like this was a joke that got made every night. This had to be Ben, Gina's husband. Yolanda had told me the two of them were live-in counselors with their own bedroom upstairs. Ben had been out somewhere with the rest of the kids in the house.

From my chair, I could see Ben as he entered the kitchen, and it made sense why everyone called him and Gina Ken and Barbie. He looked nothing like Ken—he was a couple of inches shorter than Gina, and was dark and swarthy—but he and his wife were both young and good-looking. They worked in social services, so Gina didn't wear makeup and Ben had a beard, but they were still just too cute for words, especially when they were kissing, which they did over the salad bowl.

At the same time, the last three of the house's occupants, all guys, descended upon the dining-room table like a herd of buffalo. Windows rattled, dishes clanked. I learned their names later, but there was Eddy, the Cute One. Juan, the Big Lug. And Roberto, the Cocky One. Eddy was probably fourteen, and Juan and Roberto were both sixteen or seventeen.

Except for Joy and Melanie, who both threw me the occasional dirty look, no one paid any attention to me. This made sense. Living in a group home, you get used to people coming and going. For all they knew, I'd be there one night or two, until a bed opened up at the place where I was really supposed to be.

"Let's *eat!*" Roberto yelled to the kitchen. "Fooooood!" He started pounding his plate and making snorting sounds, and Juan and Eddy joined in.

Ben stuck his head into the dining room. "It's coming, it's coming, keep your pants on." Then Ben spotted me. "Hi, I'm Ben, the assistant zookeeper. You Lucy?"

I didn't get a chance to answer because the other kids had suddenly started laughing and whooping it up. Ben and I turned to see that Roberto had leaped up onto his chair and whipped open the front of his baggy jeans. Now he was wiggling his hips like a go-go boy, and his pants fell down around his thighs, showing us his boxers. Ben had told Roberto to keep his pants on, but he'd decided to take them off. Now Melanie was shrieking, "Take it off! Take it off!" and someone else was humming stripper music. The entire room had gone from zero to sixty in five seconds.

Just so you know, I wasn't shocked or surprised to see Roberto taking off his pants. Kids in group homes tend to be pretty literal. And like I said before, dinnertime can get kind of wild.

Roberto was still swaying and just starting to slip his boxers down when Ben said, "Roberto, how the hell do you expect us to eat after seeing your pimply ass?"

Everyone laughed except Roberto, who didn't even smile. In fact, he looked downright pissed. This was his joke, and he didn't like being interrupted. That's when I knew Roberto wasn't just the Cocky One. He was also the Hothead.

Ben said, "I'll get the food," and headed back into the kitchen to get the lasagna. Roberto had to know he couldn't compete with dinner, because he pulled up his pants and sat down again, only a little bit sulky. This was also pretty typical of group homes. Things start suddenly, but they often peter out just as fast. It's the plus side of thirty-second attention spans.

I sat and watched the kids around the table. There was the usual spitting of milk and flinging of silverware, and I learned that Melanie had a crush on Eddy, but not the other way around, and that Juan was jealous of Roberto, and that the guys all picked on Damon and the girls all picked on Yolanda.

When Ben, Gina, and Leon started bringing in dinner, I watched them too. After eight years in The System, I was sure what they were thinking. Damaged goods. That's how they saw us. And when something is beyond repair, you don't bother trying to fix it. If you can't throw it out, then you store it somewhere out of the way, in a basement or storage shed where no one ever goes. Kindle Home didn't look much like a storage shed, but that's what it was—a storage shed for broken teenagers. That's why the counselors didn't even care that, under the table, Roberto and Eddy were whaling away at Damon with their feet.

"Hey, Damon," Gina said, casually serving up the lasagna. "Thanks for your help today with my computer. I'd be lost without you. What does PPP stand for again?"

"Point-to-point protocol," Damon said.

There was a brief moment of silence around the table, and I saw Gina wink at Damon. That's when I knew what she'd said had been no accident. She was helping Damon with Roberto and Eddy. She was saying to them, Lay off the kid or maybe he won't help you the next time you guys need help with the computer. But she was doing it without calling attention to herself. It was actually pretty clever.

"Pass the grub!" Roberto said.

"Man, this house sucks," Eddy said. "When are we getting cable?"

I couldn't help but notice that they'd both stopped kicking Damon under the table.

At the same time, Leon plopped a plate down in front of me. "Allergic to cheese, right? We made one with soy cheese."

Okay, I thought to myself, so maybe I'd been a little bit wrong. Maybe Kindle Home wasn't *exactly* like every other group home I'd ever lived in.

3

"Can I ask you a question?" I said to Yolanda later that night, after we'd gone to bed and turned out the lights.

"I guess," Yolanda said.

"Is this place always like this?"

"Like what?"

"I don't know. It just seems different from the other group homes I've been in." Earlier that evening, we'd played board games. There had only been two throwings of the Pictionary board. This may not sound that great, but compared to other group homes, it was. Trust me on this.

"I guess," Yolanda said. She thought for a second, and I expected her to say something about Kindle Home. Instead, she said, "Do you ever think about your parents?"

"No." It was the truth.

"I do," she said. No kidding, I thought to myself. From what I'd seen so far, that was *all* she thought about. "I miss 'em."

"What happens when someone has a meltdown?" I said. A meltdown is just like it sounds. It's when some kid completely loses control. Throwing the Pictionary board because you're losing the game is not a meltdown, but breaking a window and using a piece of the broken glass to attack a counselor is.

"It depends," Yolanda said. "When Eric stabbed Juan with a screwdriver, they had to call the cops."

"What'd they do to him?"

"Eric? They sent him to some island."

So the stories were all true. Kindle Home really *was* the Last Chance Texaco.

"And then there was Monica. She kept cutting herself with staples and paper clips. They sent her to the island too. And Brian. Melanie said that Brian tried to rape her, but everyone knew she'd been screwing him all along, and she was just jealous that he liked Monica."

Okay, I thought. I get the picture.

"Do you have any brothers or sisters?" Yolanda asked.

"No," I said. This was a lie. I'd had both a brother

and a sister. My brother had been killed in the car accident with my parents, but my sister had lived. In the years after the accident, I used to dream that she and I would run off to live in this perfect little cabin up in the mountains—I guess because I was reading *Heidi* the night before my parents were killed. In my mind, like in the book, the cabin had a sleeping loft and a big stone fireplace, and it was perched on a rocky cliff overlooking jagged, snow-covered peaks and fields of goats and wildflowers. But then my sister had been adopted, and she'd moved into a real house. For a while, her new parents were going to adopt me too, but they'd eventually decided I was too much to handle. A little while later, they'd had to move to another state, and I hadn't heard much from my sister since then.

"I wish I had a brother or a sister," Yolanda said. "It was just my parents and me."

"How many chances do they give you?" I said. "Before they send you to the island?"

Yolanda thought for a second, and I was afraid she was going to say something else about her family. "I don't know. They've never sent anyone right away. Not unless they're really violent."

"Who makes the decision?"

Just then the door opened, and light spilled into the bedroom from the hallway. I immediately closed my eyes, and not just because the light was so bright. This was a night spot check. They're real big on knowing where everyone is at all times in group homes, so there are no locks on any of the bedroom doors, and counselors do random spot checks all night long. That way, they can make sure no one is sneaking into any of the other bedrooms to have sex, which is a really big deal, or sneaking away from the house at night, which is an even bigger deal. I heard the squeak of the floorboards, and I knew whichever counselor had opened the door was now walking across the room for a closer view. A second later, a shadow blocked the light in my eyelids, and I knew the counselor was standing right over me, making sure it really was me in my bed. Then the counselor turned to check on Yolanda. I opened my eyes just a slit and recognized Ben's back and butt. Yeah, some-times guy counselors have to check on a girl's room, and yeah, sometimes they catch you dressing or worse. But you get used to the lack of privacy, just like you get used to everything else.

The floorboards squeaked again, and I saw Ben heading for the hallway again. A second later he closed the door, leaving Yolanda and me in the dark again.

I had a hundred other questions to ask my roommate, but the door had barely closed when she said, "We did have two cats. Did you have any pets?"

When I went down to the kitchen the next morning, fists were flying. But it wasn't a fight. It was an old woman kneading dough. She had her back turned toward me, but I knew this had to be Mrs. Morgan, the only counselor I hadn't met yet. It was midmorning, and the rest of the kids in the house had gone off to school. But Kindle Home was in a different district than Bradley Home, and I hadn't been signed up for classes at my new school yet. So I'd slept in, and now Mrs. Morgan and I had the house to ourselves.

"Hey," I said, still standing in the doorway.

Mrs. Morgan glanced back at me. She was old, but she was no grandma. Yeah, she had wrinkles and white hair cut short like a nun or a lesbian. And she had liver spots and sensible shoes. But she also had eyes that were crystal blue, and the kind of perfect posture that makes you stand up a little straighter, even though you don't normally give a rip about things like posture.

She stepped away from the counter, revealing a large metal bowl. "Take over," she said.

"What?" I said.

"Come here and take over this dough. When we're done here, I'll make you some breakfast."

I stepped closer. There was an enormous blob of white dough in the middle of the bowl. I'd never kneaded anything before, and I didn't want to start now. I wanted food and a shower.

"Go ahead," Mrs. Morgan said. "But wash your hands first."

I ran my hands under the faucet, then gave the dough a few feeble pokes. It seemed pliable at first, but it wasn't really. Under the surface, it was stiff. You could push it, but it pushed back, stubborn-like.

"Fold it over," Mrs. Morgan said. "Like this." She demonstrated, and I saw that she had hands like the roots of an old oak tree. I wondered how much of her life she'd wasted kneading dough. Hadn't she heard about bakeries? But I had to admit, the dough went where Mrs. Morgan pushed it and stayed there.

I tried to do what she'd done.

"Harder," she said. "And always in only one direction."

I tried again. Mrs. Morgan just watched my

hands. She didn't say anything, so I guess that meant I was doing it right.

"I'm Mrs. Morgan," she said.

"Lucy," I said.

"I'm going to go over the house rules with you."

"Yeah, I know."

She kept watching, only now it seemed like she was watching more than just my hands. Suddenly, I was glad I hadn't showered or changed out of my bathrobe. If she didn't like it, that was her problem.

"Okay," she said at last. "Stop kneading. Now we have to roll them into shape."

"What are you making? Isn't this bread?"

"No, it's soft pretzels. So we have to roll it out into ropes and twist them into shape."

I didn't want to roll it out into ropes and twist it into shape! I wanted to eat breakfast and then maybe watch some television. How often did I get a day off? But I watched as Mrs. Morgan scooped up a gob of dough and began rolling it between her hands. In ten seconds, she'd whipped out a cord of dough about two feet long and about half an inch thick. Then she placed it on the counter and twisted it into a big pretzel, like the kind you'd buy at a movie theater if they weren't so damn expensive.

"Now you try," she said.

I sighed and reached for a hunk of dough. I rolled it into a two-foot rope between my palms, but it immediately shrank back to about half that size.

"You have to be tough," Mrs. Morgan said. "Make it go where you want it to go. If you force it hard enough, it'll stay."

I tried it again, forcing it this time, and it sort of worked.

"Now twist it," Mrs. Morgan said. It was almost a command. What was she, the Kindle Home drill sergeant?

I twisted it. Of course, it didn't stay in the right shape.

"Press it down," Mrs. Morgan said, starting in on her next pretzel. "Be firm with it."

We kept rolling and twisting, and I got better. While we worked, Mrs. Morgan went over the house rules. I won't bore you with them all. Basically, they were divided into two categories. There were the Rules and Regulations, which were all the picky little things you had to do or not do, like weekly chores and not smoking in the house. If you broke these rules, you got points, which were totaled up at the end of the week. The more points you had, the fewer privileges you got the following week—privileges like being allowed to watch television or go to a football game. If you did something especially good, or if you did extra chores, you could also earn tokens, which you could exchange for money or use to buy down your point total.

Then there were what Mrs. Morgan called the Mortal Sins. These were the really important rules, like no weapons or drugs or sex and no sneaking out of the house at night. Break these rules, she said, and you could get kicked out of Kindle Home. She didn't say where kids went when they got kicked out of the house, but she didn't need to. I already knew.

"Any questions?" Mrs. Morgan said when she was done.

"Yeah," I said. "Now do we bake them?" Just as she'd finished going over the rules, we'd also finished rolling out all the dough and twisting it into pretzels.

"No," Mrs. Morgan said. "We boil them first and then glaze them with egg whites. Then we bake them. But I meant questions about the rules."

"Oh." I felt stupid. "No."

She turned toward the stove, where she already had a big pot of water boiling.

It was only then that I realized I'd forgotten about being hungry and wanting a shower. I'd never made pretzels before, and it was really kind of interesting.

"Okay," Mrs. Morgan said. "Hand me the first pretzel."

I gave her one. The adults at Kindle Home were all pretty different, I had decided. But none of them seemed too bad.

That's what I was thinking then. Of course, that was before I met Emil.

That afternoon, I was alone in my bedroom reading when someone knocked on the door. I'd long since learned that counselors got suspicious whenever they saw a kid doing anything really unusual, like reading a novel, so I slipped the book under my bedspread.

"Yeah?" I said.

Mrs. Morgan opened the door. "Time for your session with Emil," she said.

Every group home has a house therapist—someone who meets with all the kids once a week in individual sessions. Just so you know, in a group home, a therapist is different from a counselor. A therapist is the person you sit with in some room and talk to about your feelings. But "counselor" is the name for the people who handle the day-to-day operations of the group home—the cooking, the night spot checks, the wrestling to the floor of some pencil-wielding kid in the middle of a meltdown. Why they're called counselors I don't know, because they don't do any actual counseling. Maybe it's like a summer-camp counselor.

Anyway, Emil was Kindle Home's house therapist, and I was supposed to have my first session with him that afternoon.

"Sure," I said to Mrs. Morgan.

The old woman led me down to the little room that used to be the library, just off the foyer. The door was closed, but there was a little bench just outside.

"Wait here until he comes out for you," she said.

I took a seat. I could hear muffled voices through the door, and I figured the therapist was in the middle of a session with one of the other kids, who'd since come home from school. I tried hard to make out the words, but it was all a garble.

Just when I'd gotten tired of trying to listen, the door opened and Juan stepped out.

His face was a complete blank. I knew that look well. I'd used it on Leon and Yolanda.

"Lucy?" said a voice, and I turned to see a man in a beige jacket and Hush Puppies standing in the doorway.

"Yeah," I said.

He stepped back into the office. "Come on inside."

Once inside, I saw he'd taken the armchair, leaving me the couch. He had a clipboard in his lap and was busy jotting down notes. "Go ahead and have a seat," he said, without looking up. "Give me just a second, okay?"

I took a seat on one end of the couch. The therapist was the kind of guy who is hard to describe unless you're looking right at him, mostly because there wasn't anything very unusual about him. He had brown hair and a medium nose and average-sized feet and skin that was white, but not quite pale. He looked liked the actors who play ordinary dads or postal carriers in the commercials on television.

I kept sitting there, minute after minute, listening to the scratch of a pen against paper. He would write, then stop and stare at what he had written, fascinated, like it was a bonfire in the night. Then he would write some more. Mrs. Morgan hadn't introduced herself right away either, but this felt different from that. This felt like I was being ignored.

Finally, he stopped writing. He made a big show of putting his notes into a file and putting that file to one side.

"There," he said. "Sorry about that. Now, then." Then he made just as big a show of reaching for a second file—my file—and taking out the papers and putting them on his clipboard. He took a long time, making sure they were lined up, perfectly even, in the very center of the clipboard.

Only then did he finally look up at me and say, "So! I'm Emil." He almost sounded sincere.

"Oh," I said. I would have told him my name again, but I knew he knew it. Since he had my file, I knew he knew everything else about me too.

"So?" he said. "What do you think?"

"Of what?"

"Well, Kindle Home." His voice was earnest and gentle—so why did he seem so impatient?

"'Sokay," I said.

"And the counselors?"

"They're okay too." Suddenly, I knew my expression was even blanker than before. The window that was my face was locked, with the curtains drawn and the shutters barred. But it wasn't my fault. I was just getting a worse and worse feeling about this session.

"Glad to hear it," Emil said, looking down at his clipboard again. "So. I've been looking over your file."

My file already? So much for building rapport.

"There are a couple of things that caught my eye," Emil said, settling back in his chair, flipping through the pages of my file. "I see you like a good fight."

"I hate fighting," I said.

"Oh? Linda Woodhorne might have something to say about that. Eight stitches and a broken index finger?"

"She started it." She *had* started it. She was a kid in one of the foster homes I'd stayed in, and she'd had it in for me from Day One.

Emil said, "Is that right? What about Moni Wright and Jessica Birgel and Jose Hernandez? Did they start their fights too?"

As a matter of fact, they had. Moni had attacked me in the showers, and Jose had jumped me from a tree. Okay, so maybe I had punched Jessica, but she'd deserved it. Of course, no therapist had ever understood any of this. So I didn't bother trying to explain it to Emil.

"I screwed up, okay?" I said. "That's why I'm

here." I *had* screwed up. Not the fighting part. The getting-caught part. That wouldn't happen again.

Emil glanced down at the file. "And then there's this Mark Wolton incident. At Bradley Home, they caught you in his room after hours. Twice. What were you doing?"

"What do you *think*?" I said. I knew I was making it sound like Mark and I were having sex. Well, why not? That's what everyone at Bradley Home thought. It was almost funny how wrong they were. Mark was gay. I'd been in his room after hours—a lot more than twice, actually—because he'd been planning to shoot himself, and I'd been trying to talk him out of it. But once we'd been caught, I couldn't tell anyone the truth without also telling them something that Mark didn't want anyone to know. So I'd let them think we were having sex, and I'd ended up with another big black X in my file. Two weeks later, Mark had ended up killing himself anyway—probably because he no longer had anyone to talk him out of it.

But Emil had already moved on to the next page in my file. "Tell me, Lucy. You clean?"

So he'd saved the best for last. My Oxy addiction. Yeah, it was a big deal, and I don't have any excuses for this one. But it was also ancient history. I hadn't had Oxies for over a year. I'd decided they just weren't worth the trouble.

"Yeah," I said.

"Yeah, what?"

"Yeah, I'm clean. You've got my file. Isn't that in there too?"

Emil stared at me, like now I was the fire in the night—but not a controlled one, not a bonfire. No, like I was a wildfire—violent, out of control, threatening to take everything down. It was only for an instant, and then his face became completely expressionless, just like mine. But it was that moment when I knew that he hated me. I didn't know why, but I knew it was true.

Emil closed the file and set it to one side. Oh, sure, *now* he didn't want to talk about my file anymore. Now that he'd used it to put me in my place.

"Lucy," Emil said, and his voice had that fake-gentle tone again. "I'll level with you."

He was very worried about me.

"I'm very worried about you," he said.

He'd seen cases like mine before.

"I've spent a lot of time around kids. And I've dealt with kids like you before."

He didn't think the signs looked good. But I was being given one more chance at this new group home.

"You've made some pretty serious mistakes," Emil said. "But you've been given a fresh start here at Kindle Home."

But he didn't think it would matter, because I was a complete fuck-up, and I'd be out of here before the end of year.

"I really want to help you," he said. "That's why I'm here, to help you."

Okay, so maybe he hadn't *said* that last part about my being a fuck-up and that I'd be out of Kindle Home before the end of the year. But that's what he was thinking. I knew that for a fact. I also knew that if Emil got his way, I *would* be out of there, probably in less than a month.

In other words, Eat-Their-Young Island, here I come.

4

The next day, Leon said he'd drive me to my new school. He told me it was so he could introduce me to the principal, and to make sure all the paperwork was in order. But he made all the other kids take the bus as usual, which told me he was looking to have some kind of bonding moment with me in the car.

For a long time, we drove in silence. I stared out at the neighborhood surrounding Kindle Home. It was an older part of town where the thick roots of giant trees tore up the sidewalks in great big chunks. I saw now that Kindle Home had once been the biggest and most impressive house in the whole neighborhood, set back from the others like a king overlooking his court. But this king had since fallen on hard times, while his subjects had moved up in the world. With their fresh coats of paint and neatly trimmed lawns, the surrounding houses ruled now.

Meanwhile, Kindle Home was still set back, making it look like the other houses were giving it the cold shoulder.

"It sucks starting at a new school," Leon said at last. "Especially in the middle of the year."

I just shrugged and kept staring out the window. I'd been right about Leon wanting to make some kind of connection with me, but it was way too early in the morning for me to start baring my soul. Still, he was right about how lousy it was to start school in the middle of the year. By early November, people would already have made their friends for the year, and no one would be in a very let's-give-the-new-kid-a-break kind of mood.

"And it's gotta be tough coming from a group home," Leon said. "I mean, word gets out pretty quick, huh?"

I glared at Leon over in the driver's seat. "You know, you're not exactly cheering me up."

He laughed. "Oh. Sorry." But the fact was, he was right about this too. At first, students and teachers treated you mostly normal. But by the end of the second day, the whole school knew that you were one of "them"—one of the kids from the local group home. They didn't know your name, but they knew you were trouble, and not just in a spit-wads and late-for-class kind of way.

A few minutes later, we pulled into the high school parking lot, and Leon turned off the engine. "High school is bullshit," he said to me.

"What?" I said. I was surprised. I'd expected him to say something like just be myself and eventually people would see me for who I really was, and everything would be all hunky-dory. That's what group home counselors always said to you on your first day at a new school. But if I'd learned anything so far, it's that Kindle Home counselors weren't like the ones at other group homes.

"It's important," Leon went on, "because if you don't graduate from high school, you're really screwed. It's a hoop you gotta jump through, and it's a really important one. But it's still bullshit. High school is about hair gel and sideburns and blue jeans and pom-poms. Most of the time, it's not about anything real. And it's not about who you really are." He looked over at me with an intensity that scared me a little. "You understand?"

"Yeah," I said. I did understand, even though it was the exact opposite of everything I'd been told all my life. It was funny how you needed to hear the truth only one single time to know that it was the truth.

I hesitated before getting out of the car. "Thanks," I said at last, and part of me actually meant it.

The minute I saw the inside of the school, I knew that I had bigger problems than just starting school in the middle of the year. Almost everyone was white.

It's not like I'm racist or anything. It's just that the only time kids in a public school are almost all white is when they're mostly rich. And believe me when I say that it's rich kids, and the parents of rich kids, who have the biggest problem with a kid from a group home going to the same school they do. I'd known Kindle Home was in a rich part of town from the look of the other houses. But I hadn't expected the neighborhood to be so rich that the parents didn't even have to bother sending their kids to private schools to keep them away from the black, brown, and red kids.

Leon and I met with the fat, bald principal, who shook Leon's hand, but not mine.

"Welcome to Woodrow Wilson High School, Lisa," the principal said to me.

"Lucy," Leon said.

"What?" the principal said.

"Her name is Lucy," Leon said.

"Oh," said the principal. Then he went on to tell me he had very high expectations for every single one of his students. After that, he spent ten minutes eyeing me and telling me how seriously the school took discipline, especially when it came to drugs and fights. So much for high expectations for every single student, I thought to myself.

"So," the principal said, finishing up, "do you have any questions, Lisa?"

I didn't have any questions.

Out in the hallway, Leon said to me, "He's an ass-hole."

"Yeah, well, he's also the principal," I said.

"You want me to pick you up after school?" he said.

"No," I said. "I'll figure out the bus."

Leon left after that. The bookstore was closed, but the receptionist in the principal's office had given me a locker number, so I made my way there. I still didn't have any textbooks, and I didn't have anything to do in the five minutes before my first class. So I just stood there at my locker rearranging the stuff in my backpack. I also thought about that stupid little cabin in the mountains, the one from *Heidi*. I wasn't an idiot—I knew it wasn't real and that I wouldn't ever actually live anywhere like it. But sometimes it made me feel better just to think about it.

Suddenly, I noticed this girl staring at me from a couple of lockers over. It wasn't the new-kid stare. It was the group home stare. Classes hadn't even started yet, and somehow word had already gotten out about me. That had to be some kind of record. I figured it was the rich-kid factor.

"What are you lookin' at?" I said to the girl.

"Nothing," she said, turning away. But as I was watching her, I spotted Joy and Melanie pointing at me from way down the hallway. They were talking to a couple of other kids and laughing. So they were the ones spreading the news about me. Yeah, it was perverse that Joy was from a group home, and here she was trying to single me out for the very same thing. But it was that whole pecking-order thing going on, with Joy trying to establish that she was top-of-the-coop.

I did my best to turn my back on Joy and Melanie in disgust, but as I did, I bumped into this girl—one of the rich gold-jewelry types with a perfect tan and hair that had been dyed a very expensive red. She smelled like chocolate-flavored bidis.

"Hey!" she said. "Watch it!"

But I'd jostled her, and the books in her arms spilled to the ground.

"Oh," I said. "Sorry." I bent down to help her pick up her books, but that seemed to make things worse.

"Jesus!" she said. "Don't touch me!"

I hadn't touched her, I'd touched her books, and just barely at that, but I backed off anyway.

"You okay, Alicia?" said another voice, from a guy with windblown hair and a mouthful of snow-white teeth. He had to be her boyfriend, ordered directly from the Abercrombie & Fitch catalog.

"The groupie deliberately hit my books!" the girl—Alicia—said. So they called us "groupies" at this school too. Couldn't anyone ever think up a more original name? "Grouper," maybe—like the fish?

"It was an accident," I said to the guy with the hair and the teeth.

"Well, I think you should apologize," he said.

I'd already apologized once. Suddenly, it seemed like I was being asked to apologize for living in a damn group home.

"I already said I was sorry."

The guy looked at me with a stare that would have frozen antifreeze. "You the new groupie, huh?"

"Yeah," I said. "So?"

"So no one wants you here. Why don't you go back where you came from?"

I can't go back, I wanted to say. That was the thing about living in a group home. There was nowhere for me to go but forward.

He took a tiny step closer, just barely noticeable, but suddenly I could smell his aftershave—no doubt something like Domination for Men by Calvin Klein. I'd smelled that scent before.

"Just stay out of my way," he whispered, black ice for eyes. "You don't want me for an enemy."

I didn't say anything. I'd long since learned there wasn't anything you could say to a threat. But I wasn't about to look away either.

"Nate, look at this!" Alicia said to the guy, holding up one of her books. "She bent my *To Kill a Mockingbird*!"

He turned to her. "Let's just get out of here," he said, and I watched them go. They were the perfect couple, I thought to myself. Fire and Ice.

They disappeared into the crowded hallway, but

even after they were gone, I heard Alicia say, "What a *bitch*!" loud enough for everyone all around to hear. It didn't seem possible that my day could get much worse.

Then I heard little titters of laughter coming from farther down the hallway, even over the commotion of the other students. I didn't need to look to know that it was Joy and Melanie, that they'd seen the whole thing, and that their little plan to get me off on the wrong foot couldn't have gone any better if they'd choreographed it like a music video.

That afternoon, after school, I walked into the living room, where Yolanda was watching television, and I immediately smelled smoke.

"Yolanda!" I said. "Don't be stupid!"

"What?" she said, looking up innocently.

"I can smell the cigarette! Right out in the open like this? You want to get caught again?"

She lifted her left hand, which had been hidden behind the far armrest on the couch. Sure enough, she was holding a lit cigarette. "Relax," she said, taking a drag. "The only counselor home right now is Mrs. Morgan, and she can't smell a thing."

"What?"

"It's true. She was in some accident or something. Ruined her smelling thingies."

I crossed to the nearest window and opened it up. "Just put it out, okay? Leon or Ben and Gina could walk in here any second. Are you trying to get yourself kicked out of here or what?"

With a sigh, Yolanda crawled to the massive fireplace, where she tenderly put the precious cigarette out against a brick. Then she slipped the half-smoked cigarette back into the pack in her pocket.

"What's the big deal about smoking inside, anyway?" I said. "Is it that hard to walk fifteen feet to the front porch?"

"I like the way it smells," Yolanda said, scooting herself back toward the television again. And suddenly, I wondered if the real reason she was so determined to smoke inside was because her parents were smokers and the smell reminded her of them.

I said, "Just knock it off, okay? I just got myself a new roommate. I'd like to keep her around for a while."

Yolanda didn't say anything. But she smiled a little, and I could tell she was flattered that someone was showing concern for her.

I didn't have anywhere else to go, so I took a seat

in one of the chairs in front of the television.

"So what'd you think of school?" Yolanda asked me.

"Joy told everyone I live here," I said.

"Yeah, I know. She just wants to show you who's boss. You just have to let her think she is."

I thought to myself, If you let someone *think* they're the boss, that usually means they *are* the boss! And that just wasn't the way I did things. On the other hand, I was now living at the Last Chance Texaco—the last stop before being sent to Eat-Their-Young Island. Which maybe meant that the way I did things wasn't working all that well.

Before I could say anything, someone kicked open the front door.

"Hi, honey, I'm home!"

Ben.

I looked at Yolanda with eyes that said, See? I told you so! She pretended to ignore me, just kept watching the television.

Ben stuck his head into the living room. "Hey."

"Hey," Yolanda said.

"Where is everyone?" he asked.

"I think Gina's upstairs in your room," I said quickly, hoping he'd leave us alone and give the cigarette smoke more of a chance to clear. The house was big and drafty, but the smell was still pretty thick. Fortunately, he took the bait.

When he was gone, I said to Yolanda, "What the hell is with them?"

"Ken and Barbie?" she said.

I nodded. "If I was married, I sure as hell wouldn't live in some run-down old house with a bunch of juvenile delinquents."

"They can't have kids," said Damon, sauntering in from the dining room with his MP3 headphones on his head and a slice of toast in his hand. I hadn't even known he was downstairs with us.

Yolanda sat upright, inspecting the top of his bread. "Hey, that's cinnamon toast! How'd you get in the cupboard? It's locked!"

"What do you mean?" I said to Damon.

"It's true," he said. "Gina's ovaries are all screwed up."

"Really?" I said, intrigued. The cold hard truth was that we group home kids lived and died for gossip about the counselors. They knew everything about us, but we hardly knew anything about them. So I loved it whenever I learned something personal or embarrassing about them. One of my happiest memories from Haply House was when someone had discovered that most of the counselors were making less money per hour than one of the kids was making working at Pizza Hut.

"Really," Damon said. "And that's why they live in a run-down house with a bunch of juvenile delinquents."

"Because Gina's ovaries are screwed up? What does that have to do with—?"

"Think about it," he said.

I did think about it. "What? You mean we're the kids they couldn't have?"

He shrugged. "Makes sense, don't it?"

Yolanda sulked because Damon and I were both ignoring her. "I want some cinnamon toast."

Before I could ask Damon anything else about Ben and Gina, someone kicked open the front door again. I immediately tensed, because somehow I just knew it had to be Joy.

Of course, she stuck her head in the living room too, and the first thing she said was, "I smell smoke."

No one said anything, and I noticed that Damon's half-eaten slice of cinnamon toast had mysteriously disappeared.

Joy stepped closer to Yolanda. "Bad girl!" she said. "Smoking inside again? I think you should be punished. Come on, hand 'em over. Matches too."

Without a word, Yolanda slipped the pack of cigarettes from her pocket and passed them up to Joy. So that was her idea of making Joy "think" she was the boss, huh? But Joy knew that none of us would report her to the house counselors, for this or any of the other things she did. Call it the Group Home Code. The way we kids saw it, it was us versus the adults, and no one ever, under any circumstances, squealed to a counselor about anything another kid did. If you did, the punishment was far worse than anything the counselors could dole out—even worse than being sent to Rabbit Island. Once, at Bradley Home, a newbie had ratted out another kid for downloading Internet porn. The rest of the kids in the house had kept him covered in bruises for three weeks, until the counselors had finally been forced to transfer him to another home— where I'd heard kids there had given him a hard time too.

Adults were always accusing us of not respecting rules, but it was only their rules we didn't respect. We had rules of our own, and we respected them a whole lot.

Having gotten what she wanted from Yolanda, Joy

turned her sights on me. "Have a nice day at school?" she asked innocently.

My eyes never left the television. "Oh, yeah. Everyone gave me a real warm welcome."

"It don't have to be like that, you know," Joy said. "Just be nice to me like my friend Yolanda here."

Suddenly, I felt like I had a starring role in some chicks-in-prison flick. I was all set to start a cellblock riot right then and there. But I heard Ben's footsteps coming down the stairs. So rather than punch Joy in the face, I casually stood up to go close the window again.

Ben stepped into the doorway of the front room. "Gina's not up there," he said, looking at me. "Did you actually see her?"

"No," I said. "I just saw the door closed, and I thought I heard her inside." Then, with Ben staring right at me, I sniffed the air twice. Joy was looking at me too, so I knew she saw me do it.

Ben hesitated, still preoccupied with finding his wife. But some part of him had noticed me smelling the air, just like I hoped. He sniffed too.

"Hey!" he said. "Who's been smoking inside?"

"Not me," I said, sitting back down to watch television.

"Not me!" Damon said.

"Not me," Yolanda said.

"Joy?" Ben said, facing her.

"It wasn't me!" she said.

Ben sighed. "Come on. Everyone stand for a pat-down. Arms up."

Ben searched us all, but of course none of us had any cigarettes except Joy—the ones she had just taken from Yolanda. As for Damon, Ben didn't find that slice of half-eaten cinnamon toast on him anywhere.

"Joy?" Ben said, holding up the lone pack of cigarettes.

"It wasn't me!" she said.

"You're the only one with cigarettes." He slipped a finger inside the pack, pulled out the half-smoked one, and felt the tip. "It's still warm."

"It wasn't *me!*" Joy repeated, even stamping her feet a little.

"*That's it!*" Ben said. "Five points for smoking, five points for lying!" He spun around to go, gesturing with the pack of cigarettes. "And I'm throwing these away! You shouldn't be smoking anyway."

My plan had worked perfectly. I'd gotten Joy in trouble, but without violating the Group Home

Code. I hadn't actually said anything to Ben, so in the eyes of any group home kid, I hadn't squealed on her. This was the plus side of group home kids being so literal-minded.

But Joy wasn't stupid. She knew exactly what I'd done.

After Ben was gone, no one said anything for a second. It felt like the moment after you light a fuse, but before whatever you lit blows up.

Then it blew.

Joy went berserk, flailing her arms and spewing spit.

"You fucking bitch!" she shouted at me. "I'll *get* you for that!"

Great, I thought. I'd been at Kindle Home for barely forty-eight hours and my list of mortal enemies now included Emil, Fire and Ice, and Joy. And they could all get me in a whole lot of trouble, each in their own special way.

Even so, it was worth doing what I'd done to Joy, if only to see the idiotic expression on her face.

Speaking of Fire and Ice, I saw them again the next day in my second-period biology class. I'd seen them in class the day before too, when they'd walked in and looked absolutely shocked to see me, like they couldn't believe a groupie would actually be taking biology and not some Science for Boneheads class. Alicia had walked by me first, still reeking of chocolate bidi smoke, and she'd done this snotty press-her-books-tightly-against-her-chest thing, like I was suddenly going to lash out and knock them down again. And when Nate had walked by me, he'd tipped over the avocado sprout on my workstation.

The next day, he and Alicia walked by me again, and Alicia did the same thing with her books. Then, when Nate walked by me, he pointed to an aquarium full of crabs in the back of the classroom and said to Alicia, "Damn hermit crabs. They don't have any shell of their own, so they have to go around stealing other animals' shells. I bet the other animals wish those hermit crabs would just go back where they came from." He may have sounded like he was talking about crabs, but I was between him and that aquarium, and I and everyone around me knew he was really talking about me, about my living in a group home.

I'm still not sure what came over me just then. It was partly what Nate had said, and what he and Alicia had said and done the day before. But it was also partly the way Emil had treated me two days earlier, and the way the school principal had been so rude to me, and the fact that for no reason at all, Joy had decided to make my life a living hell. It suddenly seemed like the whole world was out to get me, and there wasn't a damn thing I could do about it.

Whatever the reason, I leaped up from out of my chair and shouted to Nate, "Go to hell!" Then I hauled off and slugged him in the face.

5

I was up Shit Creek. Hell, I was floating in a shit raft just above the gigantic shit waterfall at the head-waters of Shit Creek.

"*Two days!*" the principal said to me after the biology teacher had hauled me to the principal's office. "You've been at my school exactly *two days*, and you're already attacking the other students!"

Nate had been brought to the principal's office too—after I'd hit him, he'd hit me back, and then we'd really started going at it. We'd knocked over a filing cabinet and ripped down a chart that showed the parts of a flower, and it had taken six sophomores and two juniors to finally tear us apart. He'd gotten in a couple of punches but had never really gotten a direct hit on me. Nate, on the other hand, already had the beginning of a very nasty black eye—a perfect match for the black ice of his eyes.

There was a lot more yelling, and Principal High Expectations directed all of it at me. "Nate Brandon, of all people!" he kept saying. "Out of the whole school, you had to attack Nate Brandon!" I said to myself, Who gives a rip about Nate Brandon? Why is he so special? But I already knew the answer. Nate Brandon was a rich kid, and a jock. They obviously got special treatment. The principal never did give me a chance to speak, to tell my side of the story. I wouldn't have bothered telling him anyway. He wouldn't have cared that Nate had said the things he'd said, or that he'd knocked over my avocado sprout.

Finally, Leon arrived. The principal had called Kindle Home right after the fight, and someone was supposed to come and take me home. For a split second, I was glad it was Leon. Then I remembered it wouldn't make any difference.

"Get her out of here!" the principal yelled at him. "Get her the hell out of here, and don't bring her back!"

"You can't kick her out," Leon said, absolutely calm.

"Why the hell not?"

"Because it's only her first infraction."

"She *attacked* a *student* in the middle of *class*!" The principal looked even angrier than Joy had the day before. I thought he was going to pop a blood vessel in his neck.

"It doesn't make any difference," Leon said. "Read your own handbook. You can't kick her out on the first infraction."

"That's not true! I have leeway!"

Leon shook his head. "Not here, you don't. And zero tolerance applies only when there are drugs or weapons involved. But there weren't any drugs or weapons. The worst you can do is put her on detention and probation."

"Well, she probably *has* a weapon! I just didn't search her!"

"So go ahead and search her. Just make sure you search this other guy too. And if you're going to kick her out of biology, kick him out, too."

"*She* attacked *him*!"

"Yeah, well, the handbook also says it doesn't matter who 'starts' a fight—all the people involved have to get the same punishment."

The principal glared at Leon. Meanwhile, from behind his shiner, Nate glared at me, and I glared back at him. There was a hell of a lot of glaring going on in that office.

"Just get her out of here!" the principal said at last. Then he looked at me. "As for *you*, you're going to have detention until the day you graduate—assuming you ever *do*! If you so much as forget to tie your shoes, I'm going to kick you out of here so fast it'll make your head spin!"

Leon didn't say a single word to me until we were out in the parking lot and inside the car. Then, before he'd even turned on the ignition, he said, "Well?"

"What?" I said.

He didn't look at me, just clenched the steering wheel and stared out the front window. "Don't do that. Don't you *do* that whole 'What?' thing! Do you know how hard you make it for every other kid at Kindle Home when you pull bullshit like this? Now I want an explanation!"

I turned and stared out a window of my own.

"God*damm*it!" he said. "I just put my butt on the line for you in there! The least you can do is tell me why!"

I didn't say anything, just kept staring out that window.

"Lucy, don't you know I'm trying to *help* you!"

I mustered a cackle. "Yeah, right." Emil had said exactly the same thing—that he was trying to "help" me too.

"What's that supposed to mean?" Leon said.

I looked at him at last. I still had some glare left in me.

"Eat-Their-Young Island?" he said. "You think this means you're going to be sent to Eat-Their-Young Island?" This stopped me cold. I'd never heard an adult refer to Rabbit Island as Eat-Their-Young Island before. Not only didn't they use that expression, they always made a really big deal whenever one of us kids did.

"Doesn't it?" I said.

"It sure don't help," he said. "But it's only your first offense. They never send a kid there after only one offense. Not something like this, anyway."

I shrugged. "It doesn't matter. It's only a matter of time."

"*No!*" he shouted, so loudly I jumped a little in surprise. "You're *not* going there! Not if I can help it."

I looked over at him again. Who the hell was this Leon Dogman guy? But as much as I'd been certain that Emil had been lying to me, I suddenly had this unmistakable feeling that Leon was telling the truth.

"But I can't keep you from going there by myself," he said, more softly. "You have to help."

I looked out the front window. The windshield was getting foggy. Finally, I said, "How?"

"You can start by telling me what happened back in that classroom."

I thought about this. I knew he was probably just humoring me. Or trying to get some dirt on me for my file that he could then use against me later on. But I still had the feeling he was being straight with me. And I sure as hell didn't want to be sent to Rabbit Island.

So I told him everything that had happened with Nate and Alicia in the hallway the day before, and what Nate had said to me in the classroom right before I hit him. The Group Home Code didn't apply to non–group home kids, so I laid it on as thick as I could while still telling mostly the truth.

When I was done, he just sat there, fiddling with his eyebrow ring.

"Do you believe me?" I asked him.

"I don't know," he said. "I just met you. You might be lying."

"I knew it." I tried to sulk, but the truth was, he

had a point. We group home kids are pretty good bullshitters.

"You said if I told you what happened, you'd keep me from being sent away," I said.

"No," he said. "I said if you helped me, I'd help you."

"And I helped you!"

"You *started* helping me. But there's still more you have to do. A lot more."

Suddenly, I knew exactly where this was heading. I couldn't believe I hadn't seen it before. I knew now we'd drive to his apartment, or maybe some hotel.

I took a deep breath. "All right," I said. "Let's go."

"Go where?" Leon's face hardened. "Not that." He hesitated, clenching his teeth. "Lucy, has a counselor ever asked you to do something like that before?"

"No," I said. It was mostly the truth.

He looked relieved, but he also kept staring at me, like he didn't quite believe me. "Look," he said, hesitating again. "Lucy, I know things have been lousy for you. But I swear to God, Kindle Home is different."

"What do you want me to do?" I asked.

"What?"

"Before. You said there was more I have to do—to keep from being sent away. So what do I have to do?"

He smiled. "Trust us," he said. That was it? That was all he wanted from me? Was this some kind of trick?

I stared out the window for a long time after he said that. For some reason, the fog on the windshield began to clear—I guess because we'd stopped talking.

Finally, I looked over at him again and spoke a single word. "Okay."

Later that afternoon, before any of the other kids were home from school, I was coming down the stairs, and I happened to stop for a second about a third of the way from the landing. Right then, I heard Leon's voice say, clear as a bell, "She was provoked." It was coming from the office just off the foyer down below, and somehow I knew he was talking about me.

"She *says* she was provoked," came the voice of Mrs. Morgan. "She could be lying."

"And so what if she *was* provoked?" said Gina's voice. "She still threw the first punch. These kids are always being provoked. That doesn't mean it's okay to slug someone."

"I'm not saying it is!" Leon said. "I'm just saying she's only been here three days, and she's under a lot of pressure. I say we give her a break."

"No one's saying we should throw her out into a snowbank," Ben said. "We're just saying there have to be consequences to her actions."

"There *will* be consequences," Leon said. "At school. She'll have detention, and she's on probation. But it didn't have anything to do with here, so I don't see why *we* need to give her consequences too."

It was that moment in the week when all four counselors were together at the very same time. And they were using the opportunity to talk about me, about what had happened that morning at school. But how was it that I was able to hear them? I'd been sitting right outside the door when Emil had been having his session with Juan, and I hadn't been able to hear anything at all.

I took a step down the stairway, and the sound of the voices faded away. I returned to the step I'd been on.

"She has so much anger," Gina was saying.

"So do most of these kids," Leon said. "So would you if you were here."

I took a step up the stairway, and the voices disappeared again. So there was something about the acoustics of the front hall, and the transom above the office door, that made it possible to hear what was being said inside that room, but only from that one single step. If you were moving up or down the steps, you wouldn't notice it at all.

I returned to the Magic Step.

"She's convinced we're going to reject her," Leon was saying. "And it's no wonder—rejection is pretty much all she's ever known. Ten different houses in eight years? And then there's the fact that her parents died when she was seven years old. That means she's old enough to remember them."

"So?" Mrs. Morgan said.

"So maybe Lucy thinks we're trying to replace them," Leon said. "Maybe that's part of why she's so afraid of letting any adult get close to her—because she's still afraid of somehow betraying her parents."

Leon knew my file, I had to give him that. But what he was saying was all bullshit, of course. Betraying my parents? Please. It almost sounded to me like Leon was bullshitting the other counselors—telling them what he thought they wanted to hear, so they'd go easier on me.

"You think that's why she punched that kid at school?" Mrs. Morgan was saying. "Because of something that happened eight years ago?"

"I don't know why Lucy did what she did," Leon said. "I bet even she doesn't know. Whatever's going on is probably all unconscious. But I do think the key to her is the fact that she's been abandoned so many times, and that she's terrified of being rejected again. So she pushes people away before they can reject her."

Leon had silenced the other counselors at last.

Then Ben laughed. "Three days, Leon! You got her all figured out in three days?"

"Hey, it makes sense to me," Gina said.

"Oh, it makes sense to me too," Ben said. "And it's not like we haven't seen cases like hers before."

"I'm not saying Lucy is a hopeless case," Mrs. Morgan said. "I'm just saying we need to be careful. We *have* had cases like her before. Remember Luke? And Ruani? And Denise?"

"I remember," Leon said quietly.

"And remember how they ended up?" Mrs. Morgan said.

Leon didn't speak for a second. Then he said, "Lucy's different."

Was I different? I wasn't so sure. But now I knew for a fact that Kindle Home was different, just like Leon had said. The counselors here didn't all see me as damaged goods, beyond repair, fit only to be locked away. And if that was true, it meant one other thing was true too.

Maybe Rabbit Island wasn't inevitable after all.

So the Kindle Home counselors really did want to help me. But what they wanted wasn't necessarily the same thing as what Emil wanted. And the following week, I had my second session with him.

"Well," he said. "I see it didn't take you long to get into the swing of things here at Kindle Home." This sounded like a snotty reference to my fight with Nate the week before, but he was writing something on his clipboard when he said it, so I couldn't be sure.

"So," he said, "you want to tell me about this fight?"

I thought about what I'd learned on the Magic Step, about Kindle Home being different from other group homes, and what Leon had said in the car, that

I needed to trust the people there. Did that mean I needed to trust Emil too?

What the hell, I thought.

"I bumped against this girl in the hallway," I said. "She said I did it on purpose, but I didn't. Then she and her boyfriend got all mad at me, and told me that I'd better watch out, that they were going to be watching me. Someone had told everyone that I lived here, at a group home, and they were all, like, 'Groupies don't belong at this school.'"

I couldn't help but notice that Emil wasn't writing anything down. Every time he had a thought about something, he wrote that down in great detail. But I guess my version of events wasn't even good enough to be put in my own file.

But Leon had put his butt on the line for me, so I kept going. "Anyway," I said, "I had them both in biology, and they kept calling me 'groupie' and doing things like knocking over my avocado sprout."

"So," Emil said. "You were feeling singled out because of the fact that you come from a group home."

I nodded. I was surprised. He'd been listening after all.

"And you think violence is an acceptable response to that?"

Leon hadn't meant I needed to trust Emil too.

"Well?" he said accusingly. "Is it?"

"No," I said. "That's not what I'm saying."

He lifted his clipboard, holding it against his chest like some kind of protective vest. "Exactly what *are* you saying?"

I tried a different approach. "I want to stay here at Kindle Home." This was true. Being at Kindle Home wasn't just about not going to Rabbit Island anymore. Now it was just as much about really wanting to stay.

"Well, isn't that just great?" Emil said, and suddenly, he was writing on his clipboard again. But something told me he wasn't writing down what I'd said about wanting to stay at Kindle Home, or even what Leon had said about my being afraid of rejection. No, he was writing yet another reason why I wasn't fit to be living among normal people, or going to school at their normal high school.

And that's when I knew it didn't matter what I thought about Kindle Home. Because as much as I wanted to stay there, Emil still wanted me gone.

6

Principal High Expectations gave me eight weeks of detention for punching Nate Brandon in the face. For one hour every day after school, I had to pick up garbage from around the campus, and each day I had to fill at least one big trash bag. And he warned me that if anyone saw me filling my bag with garbage from the Dumpsters, then I'd get four *more* weeks of detention.

That was the bad news. The good news was that Nate Brandon was also given eight weeks of detention doing the very same thing. I was positive that if the principal had had his way, Nate Brandon wouldn't have gotten any detention at all. But Leon had said that stuff about it not mattering who "started" a fight—that all the people involved had to get the exact same punishment. And I think Principal High Expectations was smart enough to know that Leon was going to check up on him to make sure he'd followed the letter of the law exactly.

At first, I thought there couldn't be enough garbage on that campus to fill one whole trash bag, much less two bags a day for forty days. But no matter how much trash I picked up, there always seemed to be more. And by the following day, it was as if I hadn't picked up any trash at all.

For the first week, I avoided Nate, and he avoided me. But the school was pretty spread out, with lots of long, low buildings, so it was impossible for us to know exactly where the other person was at all times.

The day after my second session with Emil, I was picking up garbage alongside the music building when I spotted a Happy Meal box pushed under some bushes. I wasn't sure who was eating Happy Meals on a high school campus, but this was a real find—with a piece of trash that big, I'd fill my bag that much sooner. I'd still have to spend the rest of the hour wandering around campus looking busy, but I wouldn't have to break my back picking up plastic lids and M&M's wrappers.

I stepped out onto the sidewalk and reached down for the Happy Meal box.

"Hey!" said a voice from the other side of the bushes. "That's mine!"

I jumped in surprise. Of course, it was Nate. He'd been going for the Happy Meal box at the same time I was. I hadn't seen him up close since our fight. When he'd learned I wasn't getting kicked out of biology, he and Alicia had both transferred to a new class.

I stood up, holding the box. "Yeah?" I said. "Then how come I'm the one holding it in my hand?"

"Get choked," he said, that familiar cool tone in his voice. "I saw it first."

"Gag you," I said. But when I took a good look at him at last, I saw the bruise around his eye. It had been over a week since I'd hit him, but it hadn't healed at all. It was this bizarre bluish-purple color, almost like it was paint, and it snaked all the way up to the bridge of his nose.

"Does it hurt?" I said. Suddenly, I really wanted to know.

"No," he said. "But it did at first. It hurt like hell."

"Oh." I wasn't sure what else I was supposed to say to that.

He started to turn away.

"Hold it," I said.

He turned and glared at me. Nate Brandon was a prick, but he didn't look as stupid as I'd thought. It was all in the eyes. He didn't seem quite as cocky as I remembered either. Maybe I'd humbled him a little. He was still way too pretty, even with a black eye and a scowl. But for some reason, with that garbage sack and that shiner, he almost looked like a human being.

I held the Happy Meal box out toward him. "Here," I said. I wasn't sure why I was giving it to him. It just seemed like the thing to do.

"What?" he said. He looked confused.

I kept holding it out. "Go on. Take it."

"What's wrong with it?" Now he looked suspicious.

"Nothing's wrong with it. I'm giving it to you. You saw it first."

Slowly, he took it from me. He was still staring at me, but before he could say anything else, I turned and walked away.

The second I kicked open the front door that night, I knew something was up. Remember that group home sixth sense I mentioned earlier? I could tell there was tension in the air, a prickle of electricity. I hadn't been at Kindle Home two weeks yet, but I'd never known it to be this quiet at four o'clock in the afternoon. Standing in the foyer, I looked over at the office and saw the door was closed. I also heard the soft murmur of voices from behind the door. This wasn't weird—Emil could have been having a session with one of the kids. So why did that door, and those voices, give me such a funny feeling?

A second later, Ben stepped through the open front door behind me.

"Hi, Honey, I'm home," he said, but quietly, not calling out like usual. I looked back at him and he didn't smile, which was an event in itself. I guess he'd also sensed that something was up.

I stepped into the living room, where Juan, Eddy, and Melanie were watching television. They all immediately glanced over at me, but no one said anything. It wasn't like I'd never walked into a room at a group home and had people not talk to me. This just seemed like a nervous silence.

I headed upstairs. On the way, I stopped on the Magic Step and heard the words "like an iceberg, where most of it's completely underwater." It was a woman's voice, but not one I recognized. I didn't listen any longer, because there were too many people at home and I wanted to keep the secret of the Magic Step to myself, for the time being at least.

I found Yolanda in our bedroom, lying on her bed and playing with some buttons. "What's going on?" I asked her. "Who's down in the office?"

"God," Yolanda said.

"What?"

"Megan Something-or-Other. The program supervisor. You know—God. She's talking to Gina and Mrs. Morgan."

"So?"

Damon answered from the open doorway behind me. "So God only comes here when it's bad news."

I turned to look at him. "What does she do when it's good news?" I asked. "Call on the phone?"

Damon laughed. "This is a group home. There's never any good news."

"What is it? What's the bad news?" I was certain he knew.

"I guess we'll just have to wait and see, won't we?" He was wearing his MP3 headphones as usual, and he punched the play button. Then—and I know he loved doing this to me as much I'd loved doing it to Nate—he just turned and walked away.

* * *

"So," Eddy said at dinner that night. "What did God want?" This was an example of one of the few things I actually liked about living in a group home: Someone always said exactly what was on everyone's mind. It's not like in some of these foster homes I'd lived in, where the families go for weeks or months with no one ever saying the most obvious things, like "Anyone ever notice that Dad is a drunken asshole?" or "Everyone knows that Renee is pregnant, right?"

Gina and Ben exchanged a glance.

"The legislature just cut our funding again," Gina said, with more than a touch of bitterness in her voice. "Gotta figure out some way to pay for those tax cuts for millionaires. If you guys learn anything at all from your time at Kindle Home, learn to vote Democratic, okay?"

"Gina," Ben said.

"Sorry, sorry," Gina said. "Strike that from the record. Everyone forget I said that."

"So what's gonna happen?" Melanie asked.

"Nothing at all," Ben said. "They'll reinstate the funding. Or Social Services'll get the money from somewhere else. They always do. Maybe we'll all have to drive down to the capital and testify again. But they're not going to close us down. Okay?"

No one said anything. I think we all played with our meat loaf at exactly the same time. Even Gina.

"Come on!" Ben said. "They're not going to close us down! Trust me. Have I ever lied to you guys?"

"Yeah," Eddy said, spearing a green bean with his fork. "You told us we'd be having a 'good' dinner tonight."

All the kids laughed except Roberto, who didn't seem to be listening.

"You wanna cook dinner tomorrow?" Ben said. "Because there's no rule that says—"

Roberto plopped a spoon into his mashed potatoes. They spattered.

"Hey!" said Juan, sitting next to him. "Watch it!"

Most of the kids laughed louder than ever, but Damon, Joy, and I all stopped laughing. I think the three of us knew what was coming next.

"Roberto," Ben said, "knock it off."

"What?" he said. "You mean like this?" He packed his potatoes up into a little mound with his hands, then took his spoon and pulled it back like a sling-shot. He swatted the top of the mound, and potatoes flew out across the table, just missing Yolanda and spattering against the wall.

"Roberto!" Ben said. "Stop!"

"Hey," Roberto said, "you told me to knock it off. Or did you mean like this?" He tipped his whole plate over, onto the floor. It bounced, and food rolled everywhere.

Like I said before, group home kids could be kind of literal. Especially Roberto, I guess.

"Roberto!" Ben said, giving him a warning shout. "Don't do this!"

"What?" Roberto said, sounding like he really didn't understand. "You told me to knock it off! So I'm knocking it off!" He slid the bowl of gravy off the table onto the floor. It figured that Roberto would pull this crap on a night we were having messy food.

Ben shot up from his chair. Gina and Mrs. Morgan stood up too. "Roberto, I'm telling you one last time! Stop this now!"

"Fuck you," he said, and he stood up to tip over the table.

All three counselors moved for him at the same time. Roberto was quick, but they were quicker. Ben jerked him back away from the table, and the three counselors all wrestled him to the ground. That's when I knew that Ben always sat no more than two seats away from Roberto on purpose.

"You *told* me to knock it off!" Roberto was yelling.

"You *told* me to knock it off!"

My very first Kindle Home meltdown.

"It's okay," Ben said to Roberto again and again. "Everything's going to be okay."

Eventually, Ben got him calmed down enough to lead him out of the dining room and into the office. The idea was to get the disruptive kid away from the rest of us as fast as possible, to keep him from being the center of attention, but also to stop a chain reaction.

There was no chain reaction that night. Maybe it was because we were all tired and hungry. Or maybe meltdowns were even more common in Kindle Home than they were in the other group homes I'd lived in, and everyone was just used to them.

"Pass the freakin' mashed potatoes," Melanie said, and Gina, Mrs. Morgan, and the rest of us kids went on with dinner as if nothing had happened at all.

The following Monday after school—two days before we got out for Thanksgiving break—I was picking up trash, and I rounded a corner and found myself face-to-face with Nate Brandon. He was looking right at me, almost like he'd been waiting.

"You tried under the bleachers?" he said.

"Huh?" I said.

"Out at the track. There's always lots of trash under the bleachers."

"Oh."

"And there was a cross-country meet yesterday. Should be a whole lot of stuff."

"Oh." I hesitated, wondering if he was setting me up. But for what? "Then how come you're not down there?"

He shrugged. "Don't have any more room." But when I looked at his bag, I saw that it was still only half full.

"Come on," he said. "I'll show you."

I thought about this. Did he have a group of goons down there waiting to jump me? But he had to know that if we got in another fight, he'd get punished too, no matter who started it. Leon would make sure of that.

I nodded once, then let Nate lead me there. Neither of us said a single word.

Out at the track field, he led me under the bleachers. He was right. It was a garbage gold mine. Lots of uncrushed aluminum cans too, which were light but took up a good amount of space.

"See?" he said.

"Yeah." Why was he being so nice to me all of a sudden? Was this his way of thanking me for giving him the Happy Meal box?

He started to leave.

"Wait," I said.

He looked back at me.

"There's enough here for both of us," I said.

He looked at me for a second. I had no idea what he was thinking. Then he stepped farther in, bent down, and started scooping up garbage.

We worked in silence for a few minutes.

"This completely sucks," he said. I was listening for any little tone of bitterness that said he thought this was all my fault. But I didn't hear it.

"Yeah," I said.

Most of the garbage was clustered in the same area, so Nate and I were working together in the same tight space. I could smell his aftershave again, and it gave me a chill.

"The people sitting here were real pigs," I said.

"No," Nate said. "Friends of mine."

"You have your friends leave their trash?"

He nodded. "You should try it."

"I don't have any friends. Word got out I live in a group home." I had that little tone of bitterness in my voice now—which was exactly the way I wanted it.

"Yeah," Nate said. "That Joy's a real bitch. What's that about anyway?"

It wasn't just Joy, I wanted to say. It was also you and your bronze-goddess girlfriend! But all I said was, "It's a group home thing."

"Figures. It's whacked."

I straightened, and almost hit my head on an aluminum support beam. "What have you got against group homes anyway?"

He reached for a Snapple bottle, tightly wedged under the lowest row of seats. "Forget it."

"I mean it! What'd we ever do to you?"

He didn't say anything for a second. Then, softly, he said, "A groupie stabbed my brother a couple of years ago."

"What?" Truth was, I hadn't expected him to have an answer for me, much less a good one.

"They got in a fight over this girl. The groupie pulled a knife. My brother still has the limp."

"Damn," I said. "Sorry."

"It wasn't your fault."

"I wasn't apologizing. I was just, you know. Saying I'm sorry it happened."

"Yeah," he said. "Me too."

I tried to think of something to say, but everything I thought of sounded like another apology. And living in a group home was sure as hell nothing to be sorry for. Still, it had been pretty cool of Nate to show me his secret garbage stash, and I didn't want him thinking I wasn't grateful.

"Well," Nate said. "I'm done." I looked at his bag. It really was full this time.

"Okay," I said. "See you. And thanks."

"Sure," he said, and left. But the scent of his aftershave lingered. It still gave me a chill, but different than before. Now it was more of a little tingle. It didn't smell quite as rancid either. Now it even smelled kind of good.

7

Something was different.

It was Thursday afternoon—Thanksgiving Day—and everyone had gathered in the Kindle Home dining room for a big dinner with all the trimmings. But something seemed different from most of the other Thanksgivings in my life. It wasn't the table, although it had been fancied up with a white tablecloth, which was actually a bedsheet, and a centerpiece, which was just a basket of hazelnuts from the yard. And it looked like we had all the same food I'd had in years past. Turkey, mashed potatoes, stuffing, yams, gravy, peas, cranberry sauce, even those little baby-corn things. So what was it that was different?

"What do you think of the cranberry sauce?" Leon asked me. "And when you answer, keep in mind I made it myself." All four counselors were there, even though at least two of them were supposed to have the afternoon off. For dinner, they'd all put on jackets and ties or dresses and makeup, and Leon had shaved.

"It's good," I said to him. It *was* good. It tasted like actual cranberries, not the purplish stuff you get in a can.

"The secret is the orange peel," Leon said.

"Orange *peel*?" Eddy said. "What'd you put in the stuffing—turkey feathers?"

"More turkey!" Roberto said.

"'More turkey, *please*,'" Mrs. Morgan said.

"Wait your freakin' turn!" Roberto said. "I asked for it first!"

Everyone laughed, even though we'd all heard Roberto's joke a million times before. I had another bite of turkey myself. It was good. Moist. It might have been the best turkey I'd ever had. But the way the food tasted wasn't what seemed different about the dinner either.

Things got quiet for a second, and Ben said, "Well, it's Thanksgiving in Kindle Home, and I can't think of any place I'd rather be."

"Me too," Gina said, smiling at Ben.

"Same here," Leon said.

"And me as well," said Mrs. Morgan.

Was this true? I thought. Were all four counselors here on Thanksgiving because they *wanted* to be?

"I can think of a place I'd rather be," Eddy said. "Do they have Thanksgiving at the Playboy Mansion?"

"Every day's Thanksgiving at the Playboy Mansion!" Roberto said, and everyone laughed again.

Leon raised his glass. "To Kindle Home."

"Fork, please!" Mrs. Morgan said to Melanie, who was eating stuffing with her fingers.

Ben raised his glass. "To Kindle Home! And to everyone who lives here." Gina raised a glass, reached across the table, and clinked it against Ben's.

The sound of clinking glasses sure got us kids' attention. Suddenly, everyone was raising their glass and clinking it against all the other glasses. We were drinking sparkling cider, and more than a little of it got spilled on the tablecloth, but I noticed that Mrs. Morgan didn't say anything about that.

"Okay, okay!" Ben said. "Enough with the clinking already."

"Save room for dessert!" Gina said. "We've got pumpkin pie."

"I hate pumpkin pie," Joy said.

"Me too," Leon said. "That's why we made a blackberry pie too."

And suddenly, I knew what was so different about this Thanksgiving. It wasn't the food. It was a feeling. But it was such a bizarre feeling that I couldn't remember ever feeling it before, at least not for a really long time.

Thanksgiving at Kindle Home felt comfortable. It felt real. It felt like home.

We may have had pumpkin and blackberry pie after dinner, but our real dessert came later, when all the kids in the house gathered for our meds. Three times a day—morning, afternoon, and evening— the counselors unlocked the medicine cabinet in the kitchen so they could give us all our pills. Everyone except Melanie had to take something—I took Paxil for anger control and carbamazepine as a mood sta- bilizer—but no one took exactly the same thing. So one counselor would hand us our particular pills with a glass of water, then mark us off on a chart inside the cabinet. Then another counselor would stand and watch us actually swallow the pills.

That night, Yolanda and I were standing out in the foyer waiting our turns in the kitchen when Damon accidentally knocked an expired water-park coupon off the bulletin board.

"Lucy'll pick it up," said Joy, standing nearby. "She's getting really good at picking up garbage."

"Get conked," I said.

"Hey, I was just complimenting you on your work. But you know, if you need more practice, I saw some dog shit out in the front yard."

I ignored her. I turned to Yolanda. "I ate so much, I may never eat again," I said, and she nodded once.

Out of the corner of my eye, I saw Joy looking at me. But after a few seconds, she turned and stared at Yolanda, thinking. Then she sniffed the air. "What's that I smell?" Joy said. "It ain't cigarette smoke. I think it's propane."

"Huh?" Yolanda said suddenly.

Joy exaggerated a nod. "Oh, yeah. Funny time of year for someone to be out having a barbecue, don'tcha think?"

Yolanda's eyes got wide.

I turned to Joy. "Shut up!" What sort of person made fun of someone because their parents were killed in a propane explosion?

She sniffed the air again. "You don't smell it?"

I turned to Yolanda. "Just ignore her." I tried to

think of something to say. "Maybe we can go to the park tomorrow."

"There's something cooking," Joy said. "But I can't figure out the meat. Is it chicken? 'Cause I smell burning skin."

Yolanda whimpered. I glanced into the kitchen at Gina and Mrs. Morgan, the two counselors handing out the meds. But they were too involved in counting out the pills.

"Maybe it's ribs," Joy said. "Nothin' like a pair of bloody ribs."

I whirled on her. "I'm warning you!"

"Or pork," Joy said nonchalantly. "But pork is the other white meat, ain't it? It don't smell like no white meat to me."

That was it! The pot inside my head suddenly boiled over, and I knew I was taking her down. I jerked back a fist to slug her. Joy must have seen me, but she didn't even flinch.

"Lucy! Stop!" It was Yolanda. She had grabbed my arm, keeping me from hitting Joy.

"You can almost hear it sizzling!" Joy said.

I tried to shake Yolanda off me.

"Lucy!" Yolanda said. "She *wants* you to hit her!

So you'll get kicked out of Kindle Home!"

Yolanda's words changed everything. It was like someone had snapped a lens over my eyes and now I saw everything in a different light. Yolanda was right, of course. Joy was purposely goading me into hitting her—and in a group home, it *did* matter who started a fight. And if I *had* hit her, I suddenly knew she wouldn't have fought back, making herself look completely blameless. She was trying to get me back for the thing with the cigarettes. The oldest trick in the book, and I'd almost fallen for it.

"What's going on!" said a voice. It was Gina, drawn from the kitchen by the raised voices. It was obvious Joy and I were facing off like a couple of feuding cats.

My fist dissolved into a handful of fingers, which I ran though my hair. "Nothing," I said, with a practiced innocence. "Why?"

"Joy?" Gina said.

Joy looked absolutely baffled by the question. "Me? No. Nothing's wrong."

Gina stared at us for a second, not fooled at all by our acting jobs. But she finally turned away. The instant she did, Joy's placid expression dissolved into a frustrated sneer. This time, I turned my back on her for good.

That night, I woke up to the sound of screaming.

For a second, I didn't know where I was, that I was in my and Yolanda's bedroom in Kindle Home. For a second, I thought I was in some other place entirely. But then I realized it was Yolanda screaming and thrashing in her bed, and the feeling quickly faded.

I reached over and turned on the light.

"Yolanda!" I said, and she jerked awake in mid-scream.

I watched her for a second, her eyes confused by the walls of the bedroom. She'd been somewhere else too.

"Are you okay?" I asked.

"What? Oh. Yeah."

The door to our room burst open, and Ben skidded inside. "What is it?" he said. He was wearing just a pair of boxer shorts, and I could see his hairy chest and how fast he was breathing.

"It's nothing," I said. "Yolanda just had a nightmare."

Ben looked at her. "Is that right?"

Yolanda nodded. "Yeah. I'm okay."

With another look at both of us, Ben withdrew to his room, closing our door behind him.

"What was it?" I asked Yolanda.

She shook her head like she was shooing away a fly. "Nothing. I don't remember."

But I knew. She'd been dreaming about her parents, about the day they were killed. The after-effect of Joy's little prank down in the foyer.

"I'm okay," Yolanda said, hunching down in bed again and rolling away from me.

I stared at her back for a second, and suddenly I remembered what I'd been thinking when I first woke up, where I thought I'd been. It was just after my parents died, and I'd been sharing a bedroom in a foster home with my little sister. She'd just woken up from a nightmare too.

Not too long after that, my little sister had been adopted, and I used to imagine that her new parents were really demons in disguise holding her hostage. In my fantasies, I'd rescue her, and we'd run off to live together in that perfect mountain cabin from *Heidi*.

Now I felt that way about Yolanda—that I wanted to rescue her, to take her away from what was making her so miserable. But there was no way to protect her from the demons in her mind, and nowhere to take her even if there was. My perfect mountain cabin existed only in my imagination.

I reached over and turned out the light. But this time, I found I couldn't sleep.

After school the following Monday, I was picking up garbage in this narrow plaza between the tennis courts and the student center, and I turned and found myself facing Nate. He was standing, garbage sack in hand, at the top of a short set of concrete steps maybe fifteen feet away.

"Hey," he said.

"Hey," I said.

For a second, we both looked everywhere except at each other. I glanced up at this big window in the side of the student center. I guess it was there so kids inside the lunchroom could look down on the action on the tennis courts below.

Finally, I sort of turned toward Nate and said, "Guess what? I just found a dollar." He'd said "hey" to me first, and it seemed kind of bitchy not to say anything back.

"Yeah?" he said.

"Yeah." I *had* found a dollar, but suddenly I felt like an idiot mentioning it to Nate. As if someone rich like him would care about a stupid dollar.

He shuffled down the steps and walked over to me. As he did, he stuck his hand into his trash bag, rummaged around, and pulled out a little white plastic canister. "I found an asthma inhaler," he said. "Still works, too." He pressed it a couple of times, and it misted.

I nodded at my own bag. "I found a floppy disk." I wasn't about to dig it out, though.

"I found a can of racquetball balls," Nate said.

"I found a tin of chewing tobacco."

Nate smiled. "It sounds like we're kids comparing candy on Halloween."

"Yeah," I said, even though I hadn't been out trick-or-treating ever since I'd entered The System. Something had always come up.

"You find anything else?" he said.

I thought for a second. Then I smiled. "Just the Holy Grail."

"The what?"

"You know—Jesus' cup from the Last Supper? That the Knights of the Round Table were looking for? It was in the parking lot next to the pool." I don't know what had gotten into me. Suddenly, I just felt like joking around.

Nate laughed. "The Holy Grail, huh? Well, big deal. I found the Fountain of Youth. It was in the grass behind the football field."

"Yeah? Well, I found the Golden City of El Dorado on the other side of the faculty parking lot."

"I found the Lost City of Atlantis."

"I found the Northwest Passage."

Nate had to think for a second. "I found the Elephants' Burial Ground!"

"I found the Loch Ness Monster!"

"I found Bigfoot!"

"I found the Missing Link!"

Nate had to think again.

"Well?" I said.

He grimaced. "I guess you win, because I can't think of anything else!"

We both started snickering. Nate was laughing louder than me, but even so, I couldn't remember smiling so much in a long time. It felt good, but a little weird, and not just because Nate Brandon was the one I was laughing with.

Suddenly, something thumped loudly against the big window just over our heads. We both started in surprise. For an instant, I thought someone in the student center must've slapped the inside of the glass in order to scare us. But then something black dropped from the window to the ground near our feet.

"What the—?" Nate said.

I stared down at it. "It's a crow. It tried to fly through the window." I glanced up at the sky and saw a mockingbird flapping away. I'd heard that mockingbirds chased crows. The other bird must've forced the crow right into the glass.

"Good thing it didn't break," Nate said.

"The bird?" I said.

"The window." He was staring up at it.

I crouched down to get a closer look at the bird.

"What are you doing?" Nate said.

"Seeing if it's okay." It wasn't. The black feathers on its head were already matted with blood, and its neck looked twisted. But at least it was still alive. It was lying on the ground, twitching.

"It's just a crow," Nate said.

"So?" I said.

"Well, you know. A *crow*."

As I watched, the crow tried to stand. But its legs and wings weren't working right. It fluttered, but didn't go anywhere. It made a noise, but not like the "caw-caw" a crow usually makes. It was more of a squeak.

"You're wrong," I said to Nate, my eyes still on the wounded bird. "Crows are really smart. They're the smartest birds by far. They hide food but always remember where. And they're social too. They watch out for each other, even share food and stuff. They also have this kind of language where they can talk to each other."

"But they're mean," Nate said. "And they pick up garbage! And don't they, like, steal food from other birds?"

"Well, they have to eat. What are they supposed to do?"

Nate kind of snorted. "Never heard anyone stick up for crows before."

I let my garbage sack slip to the ground. Then I took off my jacket and handed it to Nate. "Hold this," I said. I started taking off my sweatshirt.

"What are you doing?"

"I'm going to pick it up and put it somewhere safe. That way, at least it won't be eaten by a cat during the night. Maybe it'll live long enough to be able to fly again."

"You're not going to touch it, are you? Couldn't it have a disease?"

"I won't touch it. That's what my sweatshirt is for."

I bent down again. Nate moved closer too, but not as close as me.

The crow wasn't even trying to flutter now. It just twitched. Not like it was scared or nervous. Like it was dying.

It twitched one more time, but then it stopped.

I knew it wasn't going to move again, no matter how long we stared at it. I'd just watched something die, and it was the saddest thing I'd seen in a really long time. Even so, I couldn't look away.

"Well, that completely sucks," Nate said softly.

I didn't say anything, just kept staring at the dead crow. A second later, I realized that Nate was still staring, but not at the bird anymore. At me.

"What?" I said.

"That really makes you sad, doesn't it?"

Suddenly, I felt cold and exposed. I stood up again and started slipping back into my sweatshirt. "So?" I said.

"So I just wouldn't have expected you to care so much about a bird."

Why? I thought to myself. Because I was

a groupie, and therefore an inhuman mons er? Suddenly, I wondered what the hell I was doing talking with Nate Brandon anyway.

I was just about to tell him to go get choked when he said, "Wait. That didn't come out right."

I still wanted him to get lost, but I couldn't very well say something snotty right after he'd basically apologized to me. So I was just about to make some stupid excuse about having to get back to work. But before I could say anything, something starting shining on his face, casting a metallic glint in his eyes. He looked for the source of that glint—something directly behind me—and his face got tight.

I turned to see what he'd seen.

For a second, the glint blinded me too. Then the light moved off my face, and I saw that it was coming from gold jewelry blazing in the afternoon sun. Of course, that jewelry was being worn by Alicia, who stared down at us from the top of the nearby steps. From her point of view, Nate was holding my jacket, and we'd been having a happy little conversation. Alicia didn't look pleased about it.

On the contrary, she looked downright pissed.

* * *

That night, I woke up again to the sound of screaming. At first, I thought it was Yolanda. But then I
heard it again, and it was coming from out in the
hall. Next I heard muffled shouting, the pounding
of footsteps, the slamming of a door, and more
screaming. I couldn't hear anything clearly, but I
knew they were male voices.

Ben and Roberto.

There was an eerie silence. I turned on the light
and looked over at Yolanda. She was sitting up in bed
too. I stepped across the room and opened the door.
Other doors were opening, every one except for the
room shared by Juan and Roberto. We were all staring out into the hallway, peering at each other, but
nobody said a word.

Suddenly, there was more screaming, and scuf-
fling, from inside Juan and Roberto's bedroom. Then
the door burst open and Gina flew out into the hall.

"Go to bed!" she shouted at us as she ran toward
the phone. "Everyone get back in your rooms and
close your doors!"

No one moved. As fast as things were happening,
it seemed like we kids were moving in slow motion,
like it was an episode of *Star Trek* and we were
somehow outside the flow of time.

"Do it!" Gina screamed.

I knew what was going on. Roberto was having another meltdown. Ben had gone in to do a random spot check, and Roberto had snapped. Or maybe he and Juan had gotten into a fight and woken up Ben and Gina. I'd seen stuff like this before, way too many times. I didn't need to see it again. I figured Yolanda didn't need to see it either. So I closed the door on it all.

I went back to bed and turned out the light. For the next hour or so, there was more shouting, and more pounding footsteps, and lots of murmuring. Eventually, things quieted down again, but once again I wasn't able to fall back asleep.

At breakfast the next morning, Roberto was gone. This time, we didn't need Damon to tell us what had happened. Everybody knew. Roberto had screwed up one too many times. He'd been sent to You-Know-Where Island.

8

The following Monday, Nate passed me in the hallway on the way to fourth period. He was with a couple of his friends, but he must have already told them about me, because he came right up to me and said, "Hey! I just remembered something else I found picking up garbage. Noah's Ark! It was at the bottom of the pool!"

I stared at him, his face as unguarded as an open garage door. But I didn't say anything, and I didn't smile at all. I'm not sure what came over me. I knew he wanted me to laugh with him, but I just couldn't.

Nate glanced over at his friends. Behind their dimples, they looked plenty confused.

Nate looked back at me and waved a hand in front of my face. "Hello?" he said. "*Noah's Ark?* Something I found picking up garbage? What we do every day after school?"

But I still didn't react. "I got class," I said. Then I stepped around him and headed down the hall.

For the rest of the day, I felt like crap. I knew I'd been a bitch to Nate in that hallway. I tried to tell myself that it was only Nate Brandon—the same guy who'd threatened me and made fun of my being from a group home. And that being friends with him wasn't worth having Alicia even madder at me than she already was. But some part of me knew that Nate had been pretty decent to me lately, and it had been lousy of me to dog him like that.

Even so, I wasn't ready to face him again. So I made a point of avoiding him when I was picking up garbage that afternoon—and I think he made a point of avoiding me too.

I took the bus home. As I stepped into the front yard of Kindle Home, I saw Emil leave the house and climb into his car, parked in the circular driveway out front. He drove a gigantic SUV that put his head about five feet above the top of almost any other car. Somehow, this just figured. I hoped he couldn't afford to make the payments on it. As he pulled out and started driving away, I noticed that his left taillight was burned out. With any luck, the greedy gas hog would get a ticket.

I still felt crappy and was in no mood to see other people, but I was supposed to check in with one of the counselors by four o'clock, the time I was scheduled to be home. So I went inside and checked in with Leon. Then I went back outside, grabbed a basketball from the garage, and walked around to the backyard. Someone had turned the old tennis court into a basketball court, but the concrete was now cracked and uneven.

I shot hoops by myself for a few minutes before I heard Leon's voice say, "Can I play?"

"Sure," I said. Truth was, I'd kind of been hoping he'd join me.

We played one-on-one for a while. At any second, I expected him to stop dribbling and ask me why I was out back playing basketball by myself. But he never did.

Finally, I was the one to stop.

"Something on your mind?" he said, wiping sweat from his forehead with the bottom half of his T-shirt. Unlike Ben's, his chest was smooth.

"Kinda," I said.

"Yeah?"

"I don't know." I fiddled with the ball. "It's just that there's this guy." Without the ring of the bouncing basketball, everything seemed so quiet. It sounded like I was shouting.

"Yeah?" he said, perking up.

"It's not like that," I said, quieter. "He's just a friend. At least, he was. Oh, hell, it's Nate Brandon."

"The kid you hit?"

I nodded.

Leon's face got serious. "What'd he do now?"

"It's not like that either."

"Well, why don't you tell me what it is like?"

So I did. I told him everything, start to finish. How I'd given Nate the Happy Meal box, how he'd shown me the garbage under the bleachers. How we'd watched that crow die by the tennis courts, and how I'd dogged him in the hallway.

Leon just listened. When I was done, he didn't say a word.

"Well?" I said.

"Well, what?"

"Don't you have any advice?"

"Yeah. Get a handle on the ball, would you? You were double-dribbling like crazy."

"I mean about Nate!"

He grabbed the ball from me and took a shot at the basket. He missed. "Damn," he said under his breath. Then he said to me, "You like this guy, huh?"

"No!" I said. "I already told you that!" But at the exact instant I said this, I suddenly remembered the smell of Nate's aftershave.

"So you're just friends?" he said.

"Yeah!"

Leon went to retrieve the ball. "So why'd you ignore him in the hallway?"

I thought for a second. I'd been trying to answer that question to myself all afternoon. I hadn't really come up with much.

"Because of all the things he said to me," I said at last. "Because he threatened me."

"But I thought you said he'd been nice to you lately. And that he'd only said those things before because his brother had been stabbed by someone from a group home."

Suddenly, Leon was pissing me off. "Because of Alicia, then! Because I know how she'll react if she sees us together again!"

He tossed me the ball, then nodded toward the basket. I took a shot, but I missed too.

I looked at him. "What? You don't think that's

a good enough reason?"

"I didn't say that," he said, going after the ball again.

"Then what *do* you think?"

He stopped and stared at me. "I think if you want to go through your whole life alone, it might be easier to just wear a sign around your neck that says 'Don't talk to me.'"

"What?" I was confused. What was he saying? That I'd dogged Nate in the hallway because I'd wanted him to leave me alone? Then I remembered what I'd overheard Leon telling the other counselors that day when I'd been listening from the Magic Step—that because I'd been rejected so much in my life, I pushed people away before they had a chance to get close to me.

"That's not it!" I said. "It's not like I want to be left alone!" I *didn't* want that. And I didn't always push people away either. I was friends with Yolanda, wasn't I?

"Okay," Leon said, lining up for another shot. "Forget I said anything." He took a shot at the basket, and of course this time he made it. The ball didn't even hit the rim. "But now I should go cook dinner."

"Wait!" I said.

"Sorry," he said. "Really gotta get moving."

Then he was gone, and I was even more confused than before. Was Leon right? Was I *afraid* of getting close to Nate Brandon?

It was only then that I sensed someone nearby— someone who had been listening in on Leon's and my whole conversation from inside a clump of overgrown shrubs on the other side of the fence.

"Damon!" I said to the bushes.

Sure enough, he stepped into view, headphones and all.

"Don't you ever do anything but listen in on other people's conversations?" I said.

He thought about it, then shrugged. "Not really."

"Well? Hear anything interesting?"

"Not really." He blew on his hands, and I took some satisfaction in knowing that while Leon and I had been running around the basketball court, he'd been freezing his butt off in the bushes.

"He's wrong about me," I said. "Leon, I mean. He doesn't know what the hell he's talking about."

"He knows a lot more than the other counselors," Damon said.

"What? Why?"

He put his hands in his pockets. "You mean you don't know?"

"Know what?"

"Leon grew up here."

"Where?"

"Kindle Home. His parents died when he was nine. His tribe is extinct or whatever. So he lived here from age thirteen though sixteen."

"*What?*" Normally I liked to know personal things about the counselors, but this felt different. This felt cheap. Gossipy. But I couldn't deny it made Leon make more sense. Why he always stuck up for me. How he seemed to understand the things I did.

"You said he lived here till he was sixteen," I said to Damon. "What happened after that? Where'd he go?"

He rolled his eyes. "You really don't know anything, do you?"

"Just tell me," I said, though suddenly I had a feeling I already knew.

"What'll you give me?"

"Forget it. It's none of my business anyway."

"Come on," Damon said. "I think you already know."

"I don't! And I don't want to know!" I really didn't want to know. Not anymore. Not at all.

Leaving the basketball behind, I turned for the house. But there was only one exit from the court, and getting there meant having to walk right past Damon.

"I'll give you a hint!" he said before I could even take a single step. "There are rabbits there!"

Damon was telling me what I'd already suspected. Leon had spent two whole years at Eat-Their-Young Island!

Eddy stopped me at the top of the stairs. "What's the password?" he said with a cocky grin.

"The password is 'get the hell out of my way,' " I said. After learning that news about Leon, not to mention the whole thing with Nate, I was in no mood for games.

But he didn't budge. He crouched down, spreading his arms, daring me to take him on. Group homes may be like chicken coops, but they're also like wolf packs, with exactly one dominant male and one dominant female. With Roberto gone, Eddy was determined to take his place as Kindle Home's alpha male.

Fortunately, Eddy was still only fourteen years old. I'd had to hold my own against much bigger guys than him, so I didn't have any problem pushing him aside.

At least he took it well. Behind me, I heard him laughing.

I turned the knob on Yolanda's and my bedroom, but the door didn't open. It was stuck. Most of the doors in Kindle Home stuck, but I'd never known my bedroom door to stick before.

I forced it, and eventually it gave way.

The light was on, and at first I expected Yolanda to be in there. But it wasn't Yolanda. There was an old woman in sensible shoes—Mrs. Morgan— crouched down next to my bed. I wasn't that surprised to see her there—counselors had done unannounced bedroom searches in every group home I'd ever lived in. I wasn't worried either. I didn't have anything to hide.

Mrs. Morgan stood up, then around to face me. Her expression looked extreme, exaggerated, like she was wearing a rubber mask.

First that mask looked angry. Then it looked disappointed.

Disappointed?

I saw what she was holding in her hand. It was a little plastic bag full of white pills.

Mrs. Morgan didn't say a word, but I immediately recognized those pills. Not because they were mine—I'd never seen them before in my life. But I'd seen pills just *like* them before, many times.

They were Oxies, the pills I'd been hooked on the year before. Someone had planted them in my room, and now Mrs. Morgan thought they were mine.

9

"Well?" Mrs. Morgan said, still facing me in my bedroom, with that little plastic bag of pills in her hand.

"They're not mine!" I said.

"Oh? Then how'd they get inside your mattress?"

It was Joy. It had to be. She'd planted those pills in my bedroom to make it look like I was using again. Taking or having drugs was one of the Mortal Sins that Mrs. Morgan had warned me about on my first morning at Kindle Home, when we'd made soft pretzels and she'd gone over the house rules. It was one of the things that got you shipped off to Rabbit Island. Joy clearly wanted me gone. And unless I figured a way out of this mess—and fast!—she was going to get her wish. But Joy had picked the one drug that was particularly hard for me to explain. After all, I used to take the damn things. But none of the kids at Kindle Home knew the details of my sordid past. How had she?

Damon. Somehow he'd read my file. And he'd sold the information to Joy. Or maybe she'd tormented or blackmailed it out of him. Either way, she'd learned exactly what she needed to know to make me look especially bad.

But even though I knew all this, I couldn't say any of it to Mrs. Morgan. The Group Home Code applied even here. No matter how much of a bitch Joy was being to me, I couldn't squeal on her—not without permanently destroying my reputation among the other kids.

"Lucy Pitt!" Mrs. Morgan said. "Answer me!"

I kept thinking, wracking my brain for something to say. But nothing came. So finally, I had no choice but to say, "I don't know. I don't know how they got there. But they're not mine! Mrs. Morgan, you've got to believe me!"

Mrs. Morgan stared at me. Now the mask on her face was one of both anger *and* disappointment.

She didn't believe me.

She turned to go.

"What's going to happen now?" I said. What I was

really asking was, Will I be sent to Rabbit Island?

"You'll just have to wait and see," she said, and with that, she was gone.

I didn't see Mrs. Morgan again until dinner that night. "Please pass the sour cream," she said to me, and I did, as if nothing had happened at all. Had I imagined the whole thing? Had it happened, but she'd decided not to tell the other counselors?

Something told me I wasn't that lucky.

After dinner, the kids and the counselors gathered in the living room to put up and decorate our Christmas tree. I was in the middle of untangling a wad of Christmas lights when I noticed that Mrs. Morgan and Leon were missing. When I glanced out into the entry hall, I saw that the door to the office was closed. Somehow I just knew that they were both inside, and that Mrs. Morgan was telling Leon what she had found in my room.

I had to know what she was saying. So while Gina and the other kids decorated the Christmas tree in the living room, I worked my way up to the Magic Step. Then I stared at the dusty chandelier while I listened to them talk.

"I will say this for her," Mrs. Morgan was saying.

"She's had almost no points since the day she arrived, and she's even earned some tokens too. But she attacked that boy at school. And now we find out she's using again."

"We don't know that," Leon said.

"But I found the pills in her mattress."

"That's just it. If Lucy really was using, you think she'd hide the pills in her own bedroom? She's way too smart for that. She knows we do inspections." So Leon was still on my side, I thought to myself. That was something anyway.

"Then how do you explain the pills?" Mrs. Morgan asked.

"Maybe someone set her up," Leon said. "Joy, probably. You said she said they weren't hers."

"That's what these kids *always* say. And Joy has no way of knowing the kind of drug Lucy was addicted to."

"Maybe she read Lucy's file. Or Damon did."

"That's impossible. It's kept locked up."

"Maybe. Maybe not."

Mrs. Morgan sighed. "Leon, I think it's great that you identify so strongly with these kids. But we have to be realistic. You know their recidivism rate for drug use."

To my surprise, now Leon sighed too. "Yeah. I do. I just hate the thought that she hasn't been straight with me."

I wanted to run down the stairs and pound on the door, shouting, "I *have* been straight with you! They weren't my pills!" But I knew I couldn't, not without making things a whole lot worse.

"So what do we do?" Leon said.

"We wait to hear what Emil thinks," Mrs. Morgan said.

"Emil." Even through the door and more than halfway up the stairs, I could hear the disgust in Leon's voice.

"Ultimately, it's his decision," Mrs. Morgan said, and I immediately thought one thing.

I was doomed.

Two days later, at my next session with Emil, he kept me waiting again while he jotted notes in Juan's file, then read them over again. Then he did that whole big production number where he put Juan's file away, then took the notes out of my file and lined them up absolutely perfectly in the center of his clipboard. Before, it had seemed like he'd done these things to show me who was boss. Now it seemed like he was doing them to punish me.

"Well?" he said, looking up at me at last. "What do you have to say for yourself?"

I'd thought a lot about how I was going to play this. If I told Emil they weren't my pills, I knew he'd never believe me. And even if by some miracle I *did* get him to believe me, he'd just want me to squeal on the person I thought had set me up. Neither of those options did me any good, so I figured why bother? All I could do was throw myself on the mercy of the court.

"I screwed up," I said to Emil, my eyes appropriately downcast.

"So!" he said, sounding like the villain in some cheesy James Bond movie. "You admit you were using!"

"No," I said. "But I'd thought about it. And I admit they were my pills." I figured it would sound more believable if I didn't give him everything he wanted.

"You had the pills in your bedroom, and you expect me to believe you hadn't taken any?"

"Okay," I said. "I'd had a few. But I wasn't hooked or anything." The point here was to make myself sound defensive, maybe a little bit in denial—exactly like a genuinely guilty person would sound. "But I'm sorry," I went on. "Really. And I promise it won't happen again."

Emil scowled at me. By accepting responsibility for my actions, I'd made it just a little bit harder for him to condemn me. Maybe, just maybe, there was hope for me yet.

"You're lying," he said. "You're very, very good at it, but I can still tell you're lying."

So Emil had seen through my act. I was a good bullshitter, but he was even better. Oh, well, I said to myself. It had been a long shot anyway.

"What's the truth?" he said. "Are you dealing? Is that it?"

I looked up at him. He had that look in his eyes again, the one that made me think he thought of me as a wildfire, violent and out of control, and that it was up to him to put me out.

"I'm telling you the truth," I said, but we both knew it was a lie, and we both knew that we both knew it was a lie.

He said, "You do know that I could have you kicked out of this house, don't you?"

Could? I thought to myself. Did that mean he hadn't made up his mind? Or that he *had* made up his mind and that he wasn't going to send me away?

"Please," I whispered, eyes on the ground again. "I want to stay. I promise I won't screw up again." In my experience, therapists could never get enough of seeing you humiliate yourself.

Emil fiddled with his pen, not nervously, but casually, like he was talking about the weather or the plot of some television show.

"You belong at Rabbit Island," he said at last, just as casually.

So that was that, I thought to myself. He'd made his decision. It wasn't the end of the world. I'd adapted to other places. I'd adapt to Rabbit Island too—eventually. Besides, I'd still have my stupid little *Heidi* mountain cabin, at least in my mind.

"But," Emil went on, "it seems that there aren't any beds available there until next week."

What was this? I thought.

"And," he said, "it seems that the counselors here think you deserve one more chance."

Leon! Somehow he'd managed to talk Emil out of sending me away! I told myself not to feel so happy—that what Emil was giving me he could later take away, and that it would hurt even more then if I let myself feel happy now. But I couldn't help it. I was just so goddamn relieved.

"Don't think you won't be punished," Emil said. "Because of those pills in your room, you have forty points."

Forty points, I thought. It was a steep punishment. It meant no television, no dessert, no parks or movies on the weekends, and plenty of extra chores. Still, given the alternative, forty points was the same as being lashed with a feather!

"But Lucy," he said in a low voice that reminded me of Darth Vader. "That's two strikes. Three strikes, you're out."

I nodded as earnestly as I knew how. "I know! I won't screw up again. I promise."

"And there's still one more thing," he said.

"Yeah?"

He watched me a second, like he was enjoying the sight of me nervous again. Then he reached down into his briefcase and lifted up a small, clear plastic cup with a lid. It was a urine cup for drug testing. You were supposed to fill it with pee, and they could do tests on it that told them if you'd been taking drugs.

"There'll be random urine tests," he said. "Starting today. And if we find that you're taking

Oxies or any other drug, you'll be out of this house within twenty-four hours, even if I have to bring a bed over to Rabbit Island myself."

That Friday afternoon, during detention, I walked into the school courtyard and found Garbage Nirvana. Someone had knocked over a garbage can, and the wind had blown trash everywhere. But Nate had found it first and was already busy picking it up.

He hadn't seen me yet, so I walked closer. "Hey," I said. It was the first time I'd spoken to him since that day in the hallway with his friends. But I'd been meaning to talk to him all week.

He looked over at me, but didn't say a word. Then he turned away and started picking up trash again.

"Mind if I share?" I said. I knew he knew I meant the garbage. There was plenty for both of us.

"Yeah," he said. "I mind." He kept working, and I noticed he made a point of facing away from me.

"Can I talk to you a second?"

He ignored me, reaching down for a Doritos bag and some wadded notebook papers. He left the scattered french fries for the birds.

"Are you listening to me?" I said.

"No," he said, which was obviously kind of a lie.

I came around to face him. He was still crouching. "Come on," I said. "Please?"

He stood up suddenly. "What is your deal anyway?" The black ice was back in his eyes.

"Huh?" I said, taken a little aback.

"I thought we were cool!"

"We are," I said. "We are cool."

"So why'd you dog me?"

"I'm sorry if I embarrassed you in front of your friends." I didn't mean for this to sound snotty, but I guess it did.

"I don't give a damn about my friends! I'm just confused! I thought it was so cool you gave me that Happy Meal box, even after all the things I said to you. That took guts. Hell, so did hitting me in class. And then we talked, and I saw you were smart and funny and easy to talk to. And when we saw that crow die, you looked so sad. It made you seem different from the other idiots at this school—different from the other groupies too. I even thought I kind of liked you! I thought you liked me too."

He kind of liked me? Did that mean what I thought it did? But what I said was, "What? I was going to be your walk on the wild side?"

Nate sighed. "Forget it. I was wrong, okay? Boy,

was I wrong! You're not who I thought you were." He stared at me a second longer, then shook his head. "I'm not even sure there's anybody home at all." He turned and started walking away. I guess he didn't care about the garbage anymore.

I watched him go. This hadn't turned out like I'd wanted at all. I'd wanted to apologize to him, but everything had come out bad. That's when I remembered what Leon had said about me trying to push people away. And that's when I realized he was right. Nate wasn't Ice. I was. Even now, I was doing my very best to freeze Nate out, just like I froze everyone out. I'd probably only made friends with Yolanda because she reminded me of my sister.

"Wait!" I said to Nate.

He stopped, but didn't turn.

"There is someone home!" I said. "And I'm sorry! I'm sorry for everything!"

Nate turned to look at me. His face had softened at last. His voice did too. "Lucy, what's going on?"

"I got scared," I said.

"Of what?"

I walked closer, until I was right in front of him again. "Everything! You and me. Alicia."

"What about her?" Nate asked.

"She's your girlfriend!"

"No, she isn't. She hasn't been that for a long time."

"What?"

"She's a bitch, okay? I've always known that. But every time I try to break up with her, she threatens to do something crazy. But I don't care anymore. So I broke up with her for good."

"When?" I said.

"Five days ago. I told her the same thing again about twenty minutes ago."

"Then—"

He let his garbage bag fall to the ground and took a step toward me. Now we were really close—closer than two people who were just friends would ever be. "What?" he whispered. I could smell his aftershave again, stronger than ever. It smelled like lilacs in bloom, fresh ink on clean paper, and the inside of a new car—the best smells in the world all rolled into one.

"But you're rich," I whispered. "And I'm from a group home."

"So?" he said.

"That doesn't matter to you?"

Rather than answer with words, he leaned forward and kissed me. His lips were firm but gentle, and cool from the outdoor air. We may have been surrounded by garbage—and I was still holding a bag of garbage—but it was the most romantic moment of my entire life.

"Nate, listen—" A third voice broke into our kiss. Alicia.

We both turned to look at her.

There was a lit bidi in Alicia's hand, but the real smolder was in her eyes. If she'd looked angry before, when she'd caught us talking by the tennis courts, that was nothing compared to what she looked like now.

10

Nate Brandon had kissed me. And Alicia had seen us together and stormed away, but he hadn't gone running after her. He'd stayed with me, and we'd spent the next thirty minutes telling each other how we liked each other, how we wanted to be together. We'd also had to keep picking up garbage, but hey, you can't have everything.

I had a strict four o'clock check-in time, so I had to leave right at the end of detention. When I explained this to Nate, he seemed to understand.

All the way home on the bus, I kept thinking about what had happened. I'd never had a real boyfriend before. I wasn't sure I'd ever felt giddy before either. If I had, it wasn't for a very long time.

Back at home, I ran into Joy in the hallway outside Yolanda's and my bedroom.

"I like your sweatshirt," she said, oh so calmly.

"Yeah?" I said, distracted. "So?"

"So give it here."

"What?" I was sure I hadn't heard her correctly.

"I said, I want your sweatshirt. Give it here."

Finally, I clued in. She did want my sweatshirt, but it wasn't really about the sweatshirt. If I'd been holding an ice cream bar, she would have wanted that. This was about Joy wanting to show me who was boss.

"Look!" I said. "I know you planted those pills in my room!"

"What pills?" Joy said, in a tone that told me she knew exactly what pills. Part of me wanted to punch her, but the thing with Nate had put me in too good a mood. Instead, I reached out to push her aside, just like I'd done to Eddy a couple of days before.

She grabbed my wrist. "I don't think you understand!" she said. "Give me your sweatshirt or you're gone!" She was squeezing so tightly that it hurt.

Only now did I finally really understand her. Emil had said I had two strikes. One more strike and I got sent to Rabbit Island. By now, Joy had to know this too. And she was telling me here and now that if I didn't give her my sweatshirt—if I didn't do absolutely everything she wanted!—she'd make sure

I got that one more strike. She'd already proved she could do it.

I was furious. I tried to snatch back my hand, but I couldn't get free. Her grip was like a pair of handcuffs. My hand throbbed.

She had me, and not just by the wrist. She'd wanted to be the group home's top hen, or the alpha she-wolf, or whatever you call it. And now she was.

I relaxed, and she released my hand at last. I was tempted to slug her even now. But I didn't. It wasn't worth it.

I slipped off my sweatshirt and handed it to her.

"That's a good girl," Joy said, like I was a child or a dog. Then, before I could move an inch, she said, "You can leave now."

Nate Brandon had kissed me—our very first kiss. But it might very well have also been our last. Because whether or not I got to stay at Kindle Home—whether or not I got sent to Rabbit Island instead—was out of my hands. It was now entirely up to Joy.

That Sunday night, I woke up again to the sound of screaming.

Not screams, I realized as I lay there in bed. Sirens.

Sirens? Yeah, they were sirens—lots of them. It sounded like they were coming from right in front of the house. Problem was, Yolanda's and my window looked out over the backyard, so I couldn't see for sure.

I looked over at Yolanda's bed. Even in the moonlight, I could tell it was empty.

I climbed out of bed and hurried to the door. I started to turn the knob when I felt it turning in my hand.

It was Yolanda, on her way back into our room.

"What is it?" I said. "What's going on?"

"There's a car on fire!" she said.

"What? Where?"

"Out on the street! Come on!"

There was a window above the landing, and that's where Yolanda led me. Juan was already there, his face up against the glass.

"There's a car on fire!" he said to us. So I'd heard.

I stepped up next to him and immediately spotted the fire trucks. Two were parked about half a block down the street, and another was just arriving. There was lots of movement and shouting all around them. Neighbors had gathered too, gaping and gawking, close but not too close to the center of it all. And rising from the middle of all the commotion, there was an eerie orange glow. The car itself was mostly blocked by the fire trucks, but you could see part of its front end, with tongues of fire licking up from under the hood.

"It's gonna blow!" Juan said excitedly.

"No," I said. "That hardly ever happens in real life."

"I can't see good!" he said. "Let's open the window!" But as he searched for the latch, I saw it had been soldered shut.

"I'm going to go find out what happened," Ben said, startling me. I hadn't even noticed him and Gina joining us at the window.

"Can I go?" Juan said.

"No!" Gina said. "Everyone stays inside."

Suddenly, Joy was at the window too. "Move it," she said to me. Unlike Ben, she hadn't surprised me. I'd expected her to show up eventually.

And I did move it. There wasn't anything else I could do. Joy squeezed in to take my place. I knew I wouldn't see anything from the windows on the first floor, so I accepted the fact that I wouldn't see anything more. But I stayed anyway, listening to the shouts of the firemen and the murmur of the neighbors.

A few minutes later, Ben returned. "It was parked," he told us all, as well as Damon and Eddy and Melanie, who had joined us from their bedrooms. "No one was inside it, so no one was hurt."

I'd never heard of a *parked* car catching on fire. For a parked car to catch on fire, someone had to *set* it on fire. But I didn't say that to Ben. If anybody else was thinking that, they didn't say it either.

"Can we go see?" Eddy said, and almost everyone else joined him with pleading cries.

"No," Ben said firmly. "It's all put out now anyway. The excitement's over, so everyone back to bed."

But I had a feeling the excitement wasn't over. On the contrary, I had a feeling it was just beginning.

Sure enough, when I got home from school a little before four o'clock the next day, I immediately felt that little tingle of electricity in the air again.

Eddy was passing through the front hall on his way to the television room.

"God?" I asked him, and he nodded. Megan, the program supervisor, was back again.

I looked over at the office door, which was closed. I heard the soft rumble of voices from inside, but as usual, I couldn't make them out.

I looked up at the stairs. Damon was standing two-thirds up, his head cocked as if listening.

I walked up to him.

"So," I said, "you know about the Magic Step."

"Of course," he said. "Now be quiet. I'm trying to hear."

I listened too.

"That's easy for you to say!" Megan was saying. "You don't have twenty angry neighbors screaming at you over the phone!"

"So everyone thinks it was one of our kids," Gina said.

"Of course they do!" Megan said. "Don't tell me you're surprised!"

"Of course I'm not surprised," Gina said. "But it's not fair. Who's to say it wasn't a fraternity prank?"

"Maybe it was," Megan said. "But that car was four houses down from here, and this is no fraternity."

"These aren't the only teenagers on this street," Ben said. "It could've been one of them. How come the police aren't interviewing *them*?"

"Because the other teenagers on this street don't all have juvenile records," Emil said, sounding cranky. So he was at this meeting too. That wasn't good.

"How do you know?" Leon said.

"How do I know *what*?" Emil said.

"How do you know the other teenagers on this street don't have police records? Because they all have parents? Because they live in nice houses? That doesn't mean none of them have juvenile records, believe me."

"I'm not having this argument again," Emil said. "The fact is, these kids are natural suspects. I told the police as much this morning."

"*What?*" Megan and Gina spoke at exactly the same time.

"What?" Emil said innocently, like he really didn't know why they were making a fuss.

"Emil, you know damn well what'll happen if the legislature gets their hands on those comments!" Megan said. "Are you *trying* to get this place shut down?"

"I was thinking of the safety of this neighborhood," Emil said, and Leon made a quiet "Humph" sound. "Which is what all of you should be thinking about too!" I couldn't see Emil's face, but I could tell he'd directed that last part at Leon.

"It wasn't one of these kids," Ben said. "I'm absolutely positive. Gina and I did spot checks all night long. And even if one of them did get up between the checks, there's still the burglar alarm. None of the kids can open any of the doors or windows in the house at night without setting off the alarm."

"And you're sure it was set?" Megan asked.

"Yes, I'm sure! And none of the kids know the code."

"What about Lucy?" Emil said. So it wasn't my imagination. Emil really did hate me.

Out on the stairs, Damon flicked his eyes over at me, but I just gave him my most mysterious smile.

"What *about* her?" Leon said, sounding like he was on the verge of an outburst.

"Are you sure she doesn't know the code?" Emil asked.

"Yes, I'm sure!" Ben said. "And even if she did, the machine keeps a record! No one turned the burglar alarm off last night. I checked."

"Well," Megan said. "What's done is done. We can't go back in time. But I hope you all realize how serious this is."

"What do you mean?" Gina said.

"I mean the legislature just pulled our funding! This isn't exactly going to make them real eager to put that funding back in."

"That's not fair!" Ben said. "There's no proof any of these kids were involved. In fact, we can prove they *weren't* involved! How many of the parents of teenagers on this block can say *that*?"

"This is politics," Megan said. "Since when does 'fair' have anything to do with it?"

I really wanted to tell Nate what had happened, but I didn't want to talk about it in the school hallway. So I waited until after school, when we met to pick up garbage.

He smiled when he saw me. "Where to today?" he said.

"Under the track bleachers?" I said. And on the way there, I finally told him what had happened two nights before.

"Whoa!" he said. "Someone really set a car on fire?"

"Yeah. And the worst part is that the whole neighborhood thinks it was someone from Kindle Home."

I went on to explain how the house had just lost its funding and that the fire couldn't have come at a worse time.

"Everyone thinks it was one of you guys just because you're in a group home?" Nate said, and I nodded. "That so completely sucks!" he said. I couldn't help but marvel at how much he had changed on the subject of group homes since a few weeks earlier.

"I don't know," I said.

"What does that mean?"

By now, we'd come upon the bleachers out at the track. I was glad to be back under there, even though I didn't quite know why. We stooped down together to prowl around underneath the seats.

"It means I think maybe it *was* one of us," I said. Ordinarily, this wasn't the kind of thing I'd admit to someone who didn't live in a group home—that a lot of us could be kind of wild. But I trusted Nate now, so I wasn't worried about what he'd think.

"It's true we have a burglar alarm," I went on, "but there's no motion detector. It just detects open doors and windows."

"Isn't that enough?"

I shook my head. "Doors and windows aren't the

only ways in and out of a house. And if you're inside a house to begin with, it's especially easy to figure a way out again."

"What about the spot checks?"

"That's easy. You just wait to leave until right after they check on you. They hardly ever check more than once every two hours—usually not even that often."

"So it really could've been someone from Kindle Home."

"Yeah, but why? I mean, everyone there has to know that Kindle Home is ten times better than any other group home in The System. Why would anyone want to close it down? At first, I thought it was Joy— that she'd set the fire so she could somehow pin it on me. But why do that? I mean, if she's trying to get rid of me, there are a lot less complicated ways than that."

As we talked, Nate and I were still scanning the ground under the bleachers for garbage. But it didn't look like there was any. Nate's friends had long since forgotten him, and the cross-country season was over now anyway. Any garbage that had been here Nate and I had picked up days ago. I'd known this, so why had I wanted to come here?

"Maybe it really was one of the other teenagers in

your neighborhood," he said. He thought for a second, then said, "Alicia!" He'd spoken all of a sudden, making me jump.

"Huh?" I said, turning. Was she there? Had she come upon us again?

"No!" Nate said. "I mean, she could've set the fire!"

"Are you kidding? She'd break a nail." The idea of that bony supermodel-wannabe setting a car on fire made me laugh.

"Lucy, I'm serious. She's nuts. And you don't know about her temper. You should've heard her talk about groupies. And that was before I broke up with her to be with you! There's no telling what she'd do."

"But why?"

"To get the house shut down! She's smart enough to know how people in the neighborhood would react. And by getting you moved to another home in another school district, she'd get us broken up. She'd be punishing us both at the same time."

Alicia? I thought to myself. Was it possible? Then I remembered how when I'd first met Nate and Alicia, I'd nicknamed him "Ice" and her "Fire." My nickname for him had turned out to be all wrong, but it would be funny—ironic funny, not ha-ha funny— if my nickname for her turned out to be accurate.

146

"Your eye," I said.

"What about it?"

"It's finally healed." I reached up and touched it. I don't think I'd ever touched anything or anyone so tenderly in my whole life.

"Yeah," he said. "Finally."

"I'm really sorry about that, you know."

"It was my fault. If I'd been you, I would have hit me too. But man, you sure were angry."

"What?" I was angry, yeah, but I didn't remember being *that* angry.

"Are you kidding? You should've seen the look in your eyes. It was like an explosion. I'd never seen anything like it. Scared the hell out of me, if you wanna know the truth."

I didn't like where this conversation was going.

"I'm scared," I said. "What's going to happen?"

"It's okay," he whispered, and then he opened his arms to me.

For a second, I thought about saying something mean or sarcastic—anything that would hurt his feelings. I knew if I dogged Nate right then, he'd probably never come back to me. But I didn't want to push him away anymore, not at all. What I wanted was to step forward into those waiting arms, which is exactly what I did. As his arms closed around me, I suddenly felt protected from the world, like I'd been packaged for shipping—bound in bubble wrap and suspended in Styrofoam peanuts. And now I knew the real reason why I'd wanted to see Nate alone, and why I'd wanted to come under the track bleachers. It wasn't to find garbage, or even to talk about what had happened the night before. It was so we could be together. I guess that meant that somehow I had changed.

"Everything'll be okay," he whispered. "I promise." Then he leaned forward and kissed me. His lips were even more gentle than my fingers had been when I touched his bruise. I kissed him back, and suddenly what I was feeling was even better than the Styrofoam peanut and bubble-wrap thing. I was with Nate high up in the mountains, in that perfect cabin from *Heidi*, and safer than I'd felt since I didn't know when.

But that night, I woke up to the sound of more sirens.

This time, I didn't need to look out the window to know that somewhere in our neighborhood, someone had set another car on fire.

11

The next morning, Wednesday, the phone in the hallway rang as I was on my way to the bathroom, so I answered it.

"Kindle Home," I said.

"Damn juvenile delinquents!" said the man on the other end. "Go back where you came from!"

He hung up on me, and I put the phone back down. When I turned for the bathroom, I saw that Gina had stepped out of her bedroom and was watching me with a grim face.

"Another one?" she asked. Now I knew why we were suddenly getting all these early-morning phone calls.

I nodded.

"Ignore them," she said. "They're just a bunch of ignorant jerks. I'm taking the phone off the hook."

She started for the phone. But before she had even reached it, it was already ringing again.

"I need to do something," I said to Nate that afternoon as we picked up garbage.

"Do something?" Nate said.

"About the car fires. If it's Alicia who's setting them, I need to catch her in the act. If I can prove that it isn't someone from Kindle Home, then they can't close us down."

"Are you serious?"

"Sure. I'll sneak out tonight. It can't be that hard."

"But what if you get caught? People will think *you* set the fires!"

Nate was right. If I got caught outside the house at night, it was all over. Even Leon couldn't help me. Sneaking out at night was a Mortal Sin even without people thinking I was setting the fires. I'd get shipped to Rabbit Island for sure.

"You don't understand!" I said. "If I don't catch whoever's doing this, they'll close the house down!" I surprised Nate with my intensity. But it was like Nate had said before, when he was talking about Alicia: If Kindle Home got shut down, I'd be sent to another group home in a different school district, or even a different city. In other words, we might never see each other again.

"But Lucy," Nate said quietly, like he was embarrassed by something. "What if you *do* catch whoever it is? I mean, what if people don't believe you?"

I knew what Nate was trying to say. Even if I caught the arsonist red-handed, it would still be my word against his. Or hers. And if that "her" happened to be Alicia, there was no way anyone was ever going to believe me over her. Which meant there really wasn't anything I could do. Kindle Home was going to be shut down, and I'd get moved away from Nate whether I liked it or not.

I couldn't think of anything to say, so I scanned the area for garbage. But the only I trash I spotted was a bottle cap and a couple of gum wrappers.

"Unless . . ." Nate said.

I looked back at him. "Unless?"

"Unless you, like, got the arsonist on video! No one could argue with proof like that! I have a camcorder you could use. It even works in low light!"

I smiled. Nate was absolutely right. With a digital camcorder, I could prove beyond a doubt that whoever was setting the fires wasn't anyone from Kindle Home. I'd still have to explain how I'd snuck out of the house in order to record the arsonist, but I figured I'd deal with that when the time came. Maybe I could mail a copy of the evidence to the police anonymously.

"I'll do it," Nate said.

"Do what?" I asked, confused.

"Sneak out and try to get the arsonist on video. There's no reason for you to come with me. It's not nearly as big a deal if I get caught."

Now I was more confused than ever. Nate was going to try to catch the arsonist for me? If he did get caught, people would think *he* was the person setting the fires. He might not get sent to Rabbit Island, but it wouldn't be pretty. Why would he risk that for my sake? Why would anyone risk anything for my sake?

"No," I said, firmly.

"But Lucy—"

"Forget it, Nate. This is my responsibility. Besides, you don't have nearly the experience sneaking around that I do. You try to do it by yourself, you'll get caught for sure."

"Well, at least let me come with you."

I thought about that. Truth was, I didn't want to be alone. Even more than that, I was secretly thrilled at the thought that Nate cared enough to want to help me out.

"Okay," I agreed at last.

"Fantastic!" Nate said.

He kept talking, mentioning a place where we could meet and offering different strategies we could use to catch the person setting the fires. I was listening, but I was also thinking two things: This crazy plan of ours just might work. And also, Is this what it means to be in love?

That night, I waited in bed with the lights out until I finally heard Yolanda snoring. Then I had to wait for the first spot check. The hard part wasn't staying awake—I was too excited to fall asleep. The hard part was not getting bored waiting. They say a watched pot never boils. Well, when you're living in a group home and waiting for the first nightly spot check so you can sneak out of the house and catch the person who's setting the neighborhood cars on fire, that spot check never comes either.

Just before midnight, the door to our bedroom finally creaked open, and Leon stepped inside to make sure Yolanda and I were both in bed.

Once he was gone, I crawled out of bed, being

careful not to wake Yolanda. I didn't bother making a dummy of myself out of pillows and extra blankets, like I'd heard of other kids doing when they snuck out at night. I knew that any counselor doing spot checks on this night would make absolutely sure that he or she saw my actual face. And if any of the counselors did find a dummy in my bed, they'd know I'd snuck out for sure. On the other hand, if one of the counselors found my bed empty, that only meant I wasn't in bed. I could still be somewhere else in the house. In other words, they'd have to search for me, and that would buy me precious time I might need in order to sneak back inside the house.

I listened at the door of my bedroom until I was positive Leon was done checking in on the other bedrooms. The counselor on night duty usually spent most of the time down in the kitchen or living room, so once I heard Leon plodding downstairs, I slipped quietly out into the hall. I was still wearing what I always wore to bed—shorts and an oversized T-shirt. That way, if I ran into anyone in the hallway, I wouldn't have to explain my being dressed for outside.

The hall light was on as usual, and I walked casually toward the bathroom, like that's where I was really going. But halfway there, I stopped at the doorway that opened onto a set of very narrow stairs that led up to the attic. The door was locked, but it was old, and I knew I could pick the lock. I had done this earlier in the day to make sure I could.

The instant I touched the doorknob, another bedroom door opened behind me in the hallway.

For a split second, I panicked. What if it was Ben or Gina? How would I explain my being at the door to the attic?

But then I remembered my backup plan, which I immediately put into effect. I turned to the linen closet, which was just across the hall. I pretended to be looking for another blanket.

I peeked around to see who had emerged from the bedroom.

It was Melanie, on her way to the bathroom. Her hair was messed and her eyes were barely open. She'd obviously just woken up.

"'Sup?" I said.

"Hey," she said, and disappeared into the bathroom.

I now had however long it took Melanie to pee to unlock the door to the attic stairs and then get it closed again.

I slipped my plastic library card into the crack between the door and the frame and started working it around, trying to unlatch the lock. Earlier in the afternoon, I'd been able to hear the lock click when it opened.

It didn't click.

I kept poking around with my library card, but it still didn't click.

I heard the toilet flush.

Damn! I thought. What now? Did I head back to my bedroom and risk waking Yolanda up? If I turned back toward the linen closet, would Melanie believe that I still hadn't found a blanket?

Suddenly, I remembered: I'd managed to open the door earlier that day, but it had an old-fashioned lock that needed a key to lock again, so I'd had to leave it unlatched.

In other words, the door was still unlocked!

I turned the knob.

Sure enough, it wasn't locked.

I pulled on the door, but it didn't open. Had I been wrong? Had it been locked again somehow?

No. It wasn't locked, but like almost every door in Kindle Home, it had a tendency to stick.

I yanked at the door. Was Melanie the kind of

person who always washed her hands after going to the bathroom? I hoped to God she was! To my relief, I heard the quiet splash of water in the bathroom sink.

I gave the attic door one more jerk, and finally, with a quiet pop, it gave way.

I pulled the door the rest of the way open, and quickly stepped inside just as I heard Melanie yank open the door to the bathroom.

At the same time Melanie closed the bathroom door, I eased mine shut too. Then I waited at the bottom of the attic steps, listening as Melanie worked her way down the hall back to her and Joy's bedroom.

Once she was gone, I started up the steps. They hadn't been this dark earlier in the day, but I didn't dare turn on a light. They hadn't squeaked so much either. In the silence of Kindle Home at night, the creaking sounded like the whine of distant sirens.

It was just as dark at the top of the stairs. But it had been easy to maneuver up a narrow stairway without light. The attic, on the other hand, was completely full of clutter—lamps and paintings and boxes and a rocking chair and a bed frame, taken apart and leaned up against one wall. I'd done my best to clear a narrow pathway on my earlier visit, but I hadn't expected it to be this dark. Somehow I had to make it all the way across the room to the window on the far side. And if I accidentally stumbled over anything, or knocked over any of the stacks of cardboard boxes, I might very well wake up whoever was sleeping below me.

I took it very, very slowly. I kept my feet planted firmly on the ground at all times, sliding them like a clumsy ice skater. Yeah, I caught my socks on splinters in the wooden floor. Yeah, I jostled into things. But no, I didn't knock anything over.

When I reached the window, I unlocked it and pushed it open. It didn't set off the burglar alarm, just like I knew it wouldn't. I'd checked out all the windows of the house earlier in the day, and this was the only one that didn't have one of the sensor thingies on it. Burglar-alarm companies never put sensors on third-floor windows. Why would they? No burglar would be able to climb all the way up here. Like I said before, if you're already inside a house, it's usually pretty easy to find a way out again. I wouldn't have been surprised if there was another way out too—from some vent in the basement, maybe.

But now that I had a way out, I had to make sure I had a way to get back inside again when the time came. In the movies, there are always amazingly strong drainpipes or ladderlike trellises running up the sides of houses. In real life, I'd never lived in a house with a drainpipe you could actually climb, or one with any kind of trellis at all, and Kindle Home was no exception. So I pulled out a rope from where I'd hidden it behind some boxes. Then I tied an end firmly around one of the attic center beams and lowered the other end out into the darkness outside the window. If anyone walked around the side of the house, they'd probably spot the rope, even in the dark. But I figured the only way anyone would be walking there at night was if they already had a pretty good idea I was gone.

The only thing left to do now was to put on some heavier clothes and a pair of tennis shoes, which I'd also hidden in that attic earlier in the day. Then I grabbed hold of the rope, tested it, and climbed out of the window. From there, it was easy to lower myself carefully backward down the side of the house all the way to the ground. The wood on the side of the house squeaked too, which surprised me, but then I'd never walked down a house before.

Finally, my feet touched dirt.

I'd done it. I'd made it out of the house without being caught. But, of course, that was just the first little part of a much bigger plan.

I ran to where I'd arranged to meet Nate, in some bushes at the end of my block.

"You there?" I whispered.

"Yeah," he said, stepping out into view. "I was getting worried."

"Sorry. I told you you might have a wait. They don't exactly do spot checks on a schedule."

"It's okay." Then he kissed me, and it occurred to me that this was the first time we'd ever been alone together outside of detention. It was sort of like the first day out of prison.

He held up something in his hand. "I got the camcorder."

"Great," I said. "Now let's go catch us an arsonist."

But fifty minutes later, we'd hunted all over the neighborhood and we hadn't caught any arsonists. We hadn't even seen anyone, except lots and lots of police cars. But there was almost no chance of our getting spotted, since the police never got out of their cars and it's really easy to hide from someone who's in a car, even if they're looking for you. We made a point of staying crouched down, usually hiding in yards behind bushes and fences.

"I should go back," I said.

"Yeah?" Nate said.

"Yeah. I have a feeling they're going to do more spot checks than usual tonight."

Suddenly, a siren sounded in the darkness. It was far away, but not that far. A second later, it was joined by a second siren. They were pretty obviously fire trucks.

We looked at each other, four white orbs floating in the moonlit night.

As we stood there, the sirens got closer.

"That's got to be another car fire!" I said. "But that means we missed whoever did it. Maybe we can head them off! They have to be hiding in the yards just like we are!"

"No," Nate said.

"What?"

"You've got to get home. Fast, before anyone realizes you're missing."

Nate had a point.

"Thanks for meeting me," I said.

"Go!" he said, and I turned and ran all the way home. There were still lots of police cars on the streets, but they were even easier to evade now than before. Now they were all heading for the fire, which was stupid, because the arsonist sure as hell wasn't anywhere near there anymore.

By the time I reached Kindle Home, the sirens were louder. It sounded like they'd stopped about two blocks over. I was tempted to go see what had happened, but there were lights on upstairs in the house, and I knew that people were waking up, that everyone had heard the commotion. I couldn't risk being away any longer.

I started for the side of the house.

But suddenly, I caught the right taillight of a car pulling away from the curb just down the street. I wasn't sure why the car caught my attention—it wasn't like it was that unusual for one of the neighbors to be coming or going, even this late at night.

It was a big car. And it had a broken left taillight.

A broken left taillight? At first, I wasn't sure why this bothered me. But then I remembered that I'd recently seen a car with a broken left taillight. I just couldn't think where.

Emil. The week before, I'd seen his SUV pulling

away from the front of the house, and it had had a broken left taillight too.

Was it possible? Could it be Emil, the Kindle Home therapist, who was setting the neighborhood cars on fire?

12

"Are you *serious*?" Nate said to me the next day after school. "You really think it's your house therapist who's been setting the fires?" It was raining that afternoon, and the two of us were waiting it out under the walkway between the art and music buildings.

"I know it sounds crazy," I said. "But you don't know him. He's a total asshole. And he definitely wants Kindle Home shut down. He hates us." But even as I said this, I thought, Does he really hate us? Or just me?

"Are you positive it was his car?" Nate asked.

"No." I explained how I'd just spotted the burned-out taillight, but how I'd seen that Emil's car had a burned-out taillight the week before.

"A lot of cars have burned-out taillights," Nate said.

"It wasn't just any taillight. It was the *left* tail-light." This came out sounding more stubborn than I'd wanted, but I figured I had a point.

"And even if it *was* his car," Nate said, "that doesn't mean he's the one setting the fires."

"Why else would he be on our street after midnight? If he'd been at the house for a real reason, he would've parked in the driveway!"

"So maybe he just stopped by to leave something in the mailbox."

What Nate was saying could be true. And even if Emil *was* the one setting the fires, I still had no way of proving it.

All of which meant that somehow I just had to get some proof.

When I kicked open the front door that afternoon, I saw every kid in the house standing on the stairs two thirds of the way to the landing. It almost looked like they'd been lined up that way for a picture. Except that no one was smiling, which made it look more like they'd been lined up in front of a firing squad. The staircase was so wide that everyone— Damon, Eddy, Joy, Juan, Melanie, and Yolanda— could stand side by side on a single step.

The Magic Step.

They weren't lined up for a picture. They were lined up so they could listen to what was being said in the office down below.

I knew right away that what they were hearing wasn't good, and not just because no one was smiling. The Magic Step was one of Damon's secrets, and the only way he'd share it with the other kids in the house was if he thought what was being said in the office was so important that everyone else just had to hear it. And that what was being said meant the secret of the Magic Step would no longer do him any good anyway.

Wordlessly, I plodded up to take my place in that lineup on the steps. Damon sort of nodded at me, and Yolanda gave me a wide-eyed glance, but everyone else was too busy staring at the chandelier, as if hoping for a glimpse of the future in its tiny crystal globes.

I took my place at the end of the row and started gazing at that chandelier too.

"Forty years!" Gina was saying. "How is it possible for anyone to be so petty for that long?"

"I don't know," said Megan, the program supervisor. "But I'm so tired of fighting them."

"So you're just giving up?" Ben said.

"I don't think you understand," Megan said. "Kindle Home doesn't have a lot of allies right now. Margaret and Frank Kindle know that. They've picked the perfect time to try to contest the will one more time."

Contest the will? I thought. And who the hell were Margaret and Frank Kindle? Then I remembered what Leon had said about Howard Kindle on my first day at the house—that his kids had never accepted the fact that their father had given Kindle Home away so it could become a group home. Just when the neighborhood was up in arms over the car fires, they must have decided to fight for ownership of the house all over again.

"So—what?" Gina was saying to Megan. "You're just going to give them the house?"

"Not give," Megan said. "Sell. If the Kindles want it back so badly, they can buy it from us. We could sure use the money."

"Then it's over," Ben said. "You're closing us down."

"I'm sorry, Ben," Megan said, and she almost sounded like she really was sorry. "At this point, my options are pretty limited."

So Megan had already made her decision. Kindle Home was being closed. This is what Damon had wanted everyone to hear, just like I'd thought.

Standing with the rest of us kids on the stairs, Joy laughed. It shattered the stillness of that foyer like a baseball through one of the leaded-glass windows.

We all looked at her.

"What?" she said with a sour grin. "This place is a dump. And they run it like a damn prison. I'm glad they're closing it down."

Joy was *happy* Kindle Home was being closed? Had I been wrong before to think that she loved it here and couldn't possibly be setting the car fires? Maybe she *liked* the chaotic free-for-all of the other group homes because they made it easier for her to take control. Or maybe she was secretly just as sad as the rest of us and this was her blustery, never-let-them-see-you-cry way of showing it.

Down below us in the office, Leon said softly, "What about the kids?"

"We'll find beds for them somewhere," Megan said.

"That's not what I meant," Leon said, and there was an edge to his voice. "I meant do you have any idea how many times some of these kids have been moved?"

"I know what you meant," Megan said. "But that's not something I can do anything about." There *wasn't* much our program supervisor could do anything about. We kids called her God, but now I saw that this was really a pretty shitty nickname for her.

"When?" Gina asked Megan.

She sighed. "Maybe as early as next week."

Gina laughed bitterly. "Tell me you're kidding! You're not actually going to kick these kids out of their home the week before Christmas!"

"Oh, God, I can imagine how all of this must sound," Megan said. "First these kids lose their families. Then, just when they start to make a new home, we break them up again. It's just one loss after another, isn't it?"

I heard a thump on the stairs above me and turned to see Yolanda bolting up the steps. I hadn't been watching her reaction to what was being said—I'd been staring at the chandelier along with everyone else—and I couldn't see her face now. But I knew what she must be feeling. She was reacting to being reminded yet again of her parents' deaths.

"Yolanda!" I whispered, but she didn't stop.

I wanted to follow her, to give her a chance to talk, and I even took a couple of steps after her. But I wanted to hear the rest of the conversation in the office even more. Yolanda could wait, but Megan and the counselors wouldn't.

With heavy feet and a heavier heart, I returned to the Magic Step.

"No!" Leon was saying. "That's not fair! He told her she could stay!"

What was this? I thought. But whatever it was, I already knew it wasn't good. I held my breath.

"Leon, my hands are tied here too," Megan said. "Emil was quite insistent. And given his recommendation, there's now a liability issue. And besides, the other group homes don't have the resources to handle a child like her. But it's only temporary. It's just until a bed opens up at Henry House on the other side of the state."

"This is wrong," Leon said. "Megan, you've made wrong decisions before, but this is the most wrong ever!"

"Leon, I don't blame you for being upset," Megan said. "We're all upset. I'm upset. But we have to think about what's in the Pitt girl's best interest."

The Pitt girl, Megan had said. They were talking

about me. When Kindle Home closed, Emil and Megan were sending me to Rabbit Island after all. Sure, Megan was telling Leon it was temporary, but that's what they always said when they sent a kid to Rabbit Island. Then no one ever saw the kid again. It seems that my last chance at the Last Chance Texaco had already come and gone.

"I know what's in *Lucy's* interest," Leon said, "and this isn't it!" The way Leon said my name made me feel like no one had ever said my name before. In spite of everything, I couldn't help feeling a little proud.

"What if the police catch the arsonist?" Ben said. "What if they can prove it wasn't one of our kids who set those fires?"

"Well," Megan said, "I guess it never hurts to hope for a miracle."

That night, I snuck up to the attic again after lights-out, then climbed down my rope into the yard. Because of the rain that afternoon, I touched down into mud at the bottom of the rope. But I wasn't about to let a little mud stop me. Hiding in the bushes and shadows, I skulked my way down the street until I found Nate in the same place where we'd met before. I quickly told him what I'd heard that afternoon—that our program supervisor had decided to close Kindle Home down.

"So now we've really, really got to get a recording of whoever's setting those fires," I said, taking the camcorder from his hands. "We've got to prove it wasn't someone from Kindle Home!"

But forty minutes later, we hadn't proved anything, except that a lot of Kindle Home's neighbors had motion-activated yard lights. We'd wandered all over that neighborhood, running from bush to tree to bush, lurking in the shadows. But we hadn't seen any sign of anyone setting cars on fire.

"What about you?" Nate whispered out of the blue.

It had been so long since either of us had spoken that I jumped a little. But even though we hadn't been speaking, I had never forgotten he was there.

"What about me?" I said.

"If Kindle Home closes down. Where will you go?"

I hadn't told Nate this part of what I'd learned that afternoon—that I was being sent to Rabbit Island. And on the slight chance that I didn't have to stay there, I'd then get sent all the way to Henry House.

I didn't answer, just turned and scanned the row of cars parked alongside the nearest street.

"Oh, God," he whispered. "Lucy, no! That's not fair!"

I hadn't said a word, but somehow Nate had known. Is this what they meant when they said that people in love could know each other's thoughts? But even now, I couldn't look at him.

"It won't be that bad," I said. "Besides, I'm used to it. Always moving on. I read somewhere that if a shark ever stops moving forward, it dies. Group home kids are like that too. We're like sharks." I was saying all this like I believed it, and Nate was listening like he believed it too, but it was a lie, all of it. My being like a shark, my not caring about moving on, might have been true a few months earlier, before I'd come to live at Kindle Home, before I'd met Nate. But for the first time since I could remember, I had stopped moving, and I hadn't died. On the contrary, I'd never felt so alive in my entire life. It would be moving forward now, so soon after finding a place where I wanted to stop, that would feel like dying.

"Lucy," he said, taking me by the arms, turning me toward him. The scent of him was overpowering, a heady musk, but I knew it wasn't his aftershave I was smelling now. It was him, the part of him that made him different from me—the part that excited me, the part that made him a guy.

"What?" I whispered, still looking away.

"I'll come with you!"

"No. You can't. No one can."

"Then I'll wait for you! And I'll write to you!"

"If you want," I said, eyes on the ground. "But you don't have to."

"But I do want to! I have to! Because I love you."

And that's when I looked him in the eyes.

"What?" I said.

"I love you. I love you! I love you."

No one had said that to me since before my parents had died. No one had ever really said it to me, not the way Nate was saying it now.

I'd never said it to anyone before either, not even as a joke. But then I'd never felt it for anyone before. So why couldn't I say it out loud now? It was like my lips were frozen solid.

Suddenly, he was kissing me. I was smelling him, tasting him, touching him, all at once. I'd never felt anything like it before. We pressed our bodies together, and I felt myself becoming more and more relaxed, but also more and more tense, at exactly the same time.

I'm not sure how long we kissed, but I think it was for a really long time. We might have kissed all night if I hadn't heard a very strange sound from somewhere nearby. Some kind of soft gurgle—a gentle *glug, glug, glug*.

I stopped kissing to listen.

"What?" Nate said.

"Listen," I whispered.

Now Nate heard it too, water gently splashing from a canteen. Except it didn't sound quite like water, and it didn't really sound like a canteen.

It sounded like gasoline from a gas can.

I looked back at Nate in alarm. Once again, we were four eyeballs in the dark. Our bodies weren't pressed together anymore, and they weren't relaxed either. Now we were just tense.

"Shhh!" he said, and together we crept through the bushes.

Peering out into the street, we saw movement halfway down the block—a hunched, shadowy figure pouring gasoline all over the hood of a car. But the streetlight was out, and it was impossible to see the figure clearly. Was it bony like Alicia? Average like Emil? Solid like Joy? I couldn't tell! In the darkness, it could have been Alicia *or* Emil *or* Joy. It could have been anyone at all!

"The camcorder!" Nate whispered, and I remembered the object in my hands.

I lifted the camera and pointed it at the figure. But even with the zoom lens, things were no clearer through the eye of the camcorder. It was too dark, and we were still too far away.

"We need to get closer," I said, even as I realized the gurgling had stopped.

I turned back toward the shadowy figure just as something sparked in the night. Nate and I both sucked in our breath at exactly the same time. Whoever it was, he or she had lit a match!

"*No!*" I shouted, and my voice echoed out into the street. I'd spoken without thinking, but I didn't regret it. Things were bad enough for Kindle Home as it was—we didn't need another car fire!

The figure turned toward us, toward the sound of my voice. But even with the lit match in its hand, I still couldn't make out a face.

The figure whirled away. But as that figure darted deeper into the darkness, it threw the match back at the car.

I held my breath, even as I held my finger on the button of the camcorder.

The match landed on the concrete a few feet in front of the car. It hadn't been thrown far enough to set the car on fire.

I let myself exhale.

Suddenly, little blue flames sprang up from the street in front of the car.

"No," I said.

"The gasoline!" Nate said. "It must've dripped from the car!"

"We have to put it out before the car catches!" I said, already fighting my way out of the bushes.

Out on the street, I ran for the car. I sensed Nate was right behind me.

In an instant, the street in front of the car exploded into flames. And an instant after that, the fire leaped up onto the hood of the car.

"No!" I shouted, but I kept on running.

"Forget it!" Nate said. "Let's get out of here!"

"No!" I said, approaching the car at last. "We can still put it out!" But how? Throw dirt on top of it? But there was no dirt nearby—just grass and gravel and concrete.

"Our coats!" I said. "We can swat it out with our

coats!" The flames had engulfed only part of the hood, and it didn't look like the fire had yet slipped down into the engine.

I whipped off my coat, even as I kept hold of the camcorder. Then I crouched down in front of the car, ready to give battle to the flames, like a gladiator with a whip.

But before I could even take my first swing, I saw a porch light flicker on. Then another one came on, and another, until there were lights rising all around us. These weren't motion activated—people were waking up! And suddenly, there was a spotlight from farther down the street. It was shining right on Nate, who was farther out in the street than I was, and it was coming from a car.

A police car.

"Don't move, son!" crackled the voice from the speaker, even as silent flames swept higher into the sky. "Stay right where you are!"

The shadows of night were long gone now, banished by the spotlight, the porch lights, and the light of the fire. The fire itself was out of control, unstoppable even with something more than a coat. The heat of the wild flames burned my naked face, but I didn't dare move away. We were trapped, Nate and I. The police had caught us at the scene of the crime. And now everyone would think it was us who had set the fires.

13

"Go!" Nate whispered to me.

"What?" I said. It was seconds later, as the car fire in front of us continued to rage out of control. Nate was still caught in the police spotlight, trapped like a bug in amber. But I was confused by what he had said. There was no way we could outrun the police—they had him right in their sight!

"They haven't seen you yet!" he said through clenched teeth. "Just me! You can still get away!"

In an instant, I saw he was right. The police were still halfway down the block. I was crouched down in front of a car, hidden from their view. I ducked down lower, hiding behind the grille and the flames. Sure, maybe some of the neighbors on their porches had seen me, or might see me, but the police hadn't, not yet. And there was a big clump of bushes nearby— part of a network of bushes and fences and alleyways that I now knew very well, even in the dark. Kindle Home was only a couple of blocks over. I could almost certainly slip away.

"But Nate," I said, "you—"

He whispered urgently. "It's too late for me! But you've got to go!"

I stared at him. The ice was back in his eyes, a frozen glare commanding me, bullying me.

"*Now!*" he said, even as I heard the static of the police radio, and the rise of sirens one block over. They had called for other cars. They would all converge in the seconds to come. If I was going to leave, I had to do it now.

I turned and dove into the bushes. I was getting so good at this that they barely rustled. Once I was hidden from sight, I scurried upright and ran.

In less than two minutes, I was back underneath the rope that led up the side of the house to the Kindle Home attic. I slipped the camcorder into the waist of my pants and started climbing.

But halfway up the wall, I happened to glance down. Since I'd climbed down an hour or so earlier, the partial moon had shifted. Directly above me now, its light was shining on the mud below. And in the flaxen glow of that moon, I saw footprints. There were my own footprints, leading from the bottom of the rope out to the front yard, and back again. But then there were two more sets of footprints, one set made by someone going from the backyard to the front, and a second set made by someone going from the front yard to the back.

Footprints? Had they been there before, an hour earlier? I remembered the mud, but I didn't remember any footprints. But there hadn't been moonlight then, so I might not have seen them even if they had been there. Still, they looked fresh—deep and cleanly treaded, clearly made since the afternoon rain. Maybe they'd been made earlier, after the rain stopped but before dark, by someone walking around the house to the basketball court.

But what if they'd been made after dark, after lights-out—even after I'd climbed down the rope an hour before? Could it be that someone else from Kindle Home was sneaking out in the middle of the night—maybe someone who had found a way to sneak out of the basement into the backyard? But that could mean it was one of us kids who was setting the fires after all! Was it Joy? It would explain her being all smiles on the Magic Step the day before.

I needed to get a closer look at those footprints, to see if they were made by a guy or a girl, and by what kind of shoe. Then maybe I could match them to someone inside the house.

But the second I started climbing down the rope again, I remembered the sirens. The house would be woken up by now, and people would soon notice if I wasn't around. And the longer I stayed dangling down the side of our house, the more likely I was to be spotted by a policeman, or by one of our neighbors hurrying by our house on the way to the scene of the crime.

The footprints would have to wait until morning. Quickly, I climbed the rest of the way up to the attic. Once there, I pulled up my rope, hid it and the camcorder and my clothes, and slipped my way back down to the second floor.

But, of course, it rained again during the night. The next morning, the footprints were gone.

That morning at school, I ran into Alicia almost first thing. I was walking down the hallway on the way to my locker, and suddenly the crowd opened and there she was, standing right in front of me.

She glared at me, gold jewelry dangling. Then,

like I wasn't even worth the bother of a bitchy remark, she turned away. But as she did, I saw the smug smirk on her lips. I also noticed she wasn't bothering to hold her books tightly against her chest anymore. Now she was holding them confidently out in front, which I guess meant she thought that I was no longer a threat to her—that she'd put Nate and me in my place. In other words, she knew what had happened the night before, what had happened to Nate. But *how* did she know? Because she had been there?

Did she also know what had happened to Nate after the police had taken him? I desperately wanted to know, but I couldn't exactly ask her. But if she knew, other people would too.

Sure enough, less than two minutes later, I walked by Arthur Pratt in the hallway and heard him say to his friends, "Nate Brandon's at Ragman Hall! The police caught him setting car fires in the North End!"

Ragman Hall was the city's temporary juvenile detention center. I'd been there a few times myself—a couple of times when I was caught doing something stupid, but mostly when I was waiting for a bed to open up somewhere else. Like on Rabbit

Island, security was really tight, basically like a prison.

I had to see Nate. So that afternoon during detention, I decided to sneak away from campus. This was risky—if Principal High Expectations found out I'd left, he'd expel me from school for sure. And I had only sixty minutes to make it all the way over to Ragman Hall, which was more than a mile away, then back again to school, and somehow fill my sack with garbage somewhere along the way. Then again, I wasn't risking that much, since chances were that I wasn't going to be at Principal High Expectations' school much longer anyway.

I ran all the way to Ragman Hall. At the front desk, I told them I was Nate's sister, because I knew he didn't have a sister, so she couldn't have already come to visit him. Plus, I knew if they asked Nate about me, he'd back me up completely. The only problem would be if Nate's real family was visiting him right then, or if someone at Ragman Hall recognized me from one of my stays there.

"Wait," the receptionist said to me. Then she called somebody up on the phone. A minute or so later, she motioned me back over and gave me directions to the waiting room. I pretended to listen, but

I already knew exactly where to go, even though I'd never had a visitor there, or anywhere else for that matter.

Nate was waiting for me in a room with orange vinyl couches and windows that were just narrow slits. He was wearing a blue jumper, and it really did look like something you'd see in prison. He looked surprised to see me, but happy too.

"What are you—?" he started to say.

"I needed to see you." I *had* needed to see him. I just wasn't sure why.

"But how did you—?"

"I'm on detention," I said. "I'm collecting garbage right now."

I stepped closer and kissed him full on the lips, even though I knew we were on short-circuit television. I doubted the person minding the camera had been told I was Nate's sister, but if he had, I figured it might spice up his day.

"I wanted to say thanks," I said.

"For what?" Nate asked.

"For taking the blame. For making me leave last night." Was this the real reason I had had to see him—to thank him for the sacrifice he had made? But even as I thought this, I knew it wasn't.

He shrugged. "It only made sense. If they'd caught you, it would've been all over. They would've sent you to Eat-Their-Young Island for sure." I'd already explained to Nate how Kindle Home was the Last Chance Texaco. "But it's only my first offense. And my dad can afford a lawyer. I'll be out of here in a couple of days. It's no big deal."

Nate was wrong. It was a big deal. Short of killing someone, fire was the biggest deal of all. Rich parents helped, but there would still be consequences for him. If other rich people complained loud enough, there might even be a lot of consequences. Depending on the judge, he could even be sent to Rabbit Island for a while. No matter what, his life was going to be very different from here on out. And it was all because of me.

"I'm sorry," I said. "Nate, I'm so sorry for all of this."

He rolled his eyes. "There's nothing to be sorry for. Like I said, this is no big deal." But even as he smiled, I saw a tear running down his face.

So Nate knew the truth. He'd been trying to lie to make me feel better. The fact was, he was terrified.

He tried to turn away, ashamed of his tears, but I pulled him toward me and took him in my arms.

Suddenly, he was crying outright, deep, wracking sobs that made his whole body jerk, like he was starting to crumble. It was up to me to hold him upright, to keep him together.

"Everything'll be okay!" I whispered. "I promise."

"How can you be so sure?" he said.

I looked at him. I knew my face was opening at last—shutters, windows, doors, and all.

"Because I love you," I said. There. For the first time in my life, I'd said it. And I knew that my telling him that was the real reason I'd had to come to see him.

I held him in my arms, breathing him in, letting him inhale me too, and suddenly I knew something else, something I had to do.

Somehow, I had to get him the hell out of there.

"So," Eddy said to Ben and Gina over dinner that night. "Is Kindle Home closing or not?"

Once again, I was glad that someone had said out loud what everyone else was thinking.

Ben's eyes went wide. "How do you know—?"

"We just do," Melanie said. "So is it happening or not?"

As usual, Gina and Ben exchanged a glance.

"Maybe," Gina said.

"Gina!" Ben said.

"What? It's their home. They have a right to know what's going on. Besides, they obviously already know."

"But they can't close us down now!" Eddy said. "They caught the guy who was setting the cars on fire. It wasn't one of us! It was some rich jock dude."

"You'd think that would make a difference, wouldn't you?" Gina said bitterly.

"It *does* make a difference," Ben said. "They won't close us down. They *can't*, not now."

I looked around the table. Everyone just sat there looking gloomy. No one was eating their tacos, not even Gina or Ben. Joy was scowling, but I wondered if she was feeling what everyone else was feeling. Maybe she was just annoyed because Nate and I had ruined her plan to get the house shut down.

"This should be a real fun Christmas," Gina mumbled.

I glanced around at the Christmas decorations. We'd really gone hog-wild, more than in any other group home I'd ever lived in. In the dining room alone, there were paper snowflakes and bows taped to the walls and little sprigs of holly from the back-yard on the bureaus, and someone had hung a big tinfoil star from the fixture above the table. It all seemed kind of ironic now.

"They won't close us," Ben said, and he deliberately picked up a taco and started eating. It crunched and crumbled in his hand. "Shit!" he said angrily, but no one laughed.

"You okay?" I said to Yolanda, sitting next to me.

"Huh? Oh, yeah." But she looked like she was going to burst out crying.

This was too much tension for group home kids to take. There would be a meltdown tonight, I thought to myself. The only question was, Which one of us was going to do the melting down?

That night, after dinner, I was alone in my room putting clean laundry into my dresser when someone knocked on my door.

When I opened the door, I saw Leon tightly gripping the two sides of the doorframe.

He said, "If Kindle Home closes, Emil's going to send you to Rabbit Island."

"I know," I said.

He stared at me for a second. "The step on the staircase?"

I nodded.

He smiled a little wistfully. "That still works?" I nodded again. "Anyway, I just thought you should know."

"Thanks." I kept putting away my T-shirts. Then I said, "Why does he hate me so much?"

"Emil? I wish I knew. But he hates us all. He hates every group home kid." I liked that Leon thought of himself as a group home kid. I thought of him that way too. But what he'd said about Emil— did Emil hate us enough to set a series of cars on fire? I thought so, but I wondered if Leon would.

"I also wanted to say I'm sorry," he said.

"For what?"

He snatched his hands from the doorframe. He'd been holding it so tightly, I almost expected the house to fall down around him.

"For Rabbit Island," he said. "It's not fair. It's *really* not fair."

"It's not your fault." It wasn't. I'd heard how he'd fought for me.

"Still. I made you a promise. You lived up to your half of it. But I didn't live up to mine." Now that Leon's hands were free, he didn't seem to have anything to do with them. So he stuffed them deep into his pockets.

"It doesn't matter," I said. "I don't care if I get sent to Rabbit Island anymore." Suddenly, I remembered my first day at Kindle Home, and how I hadn't wanted to unpack my clothes in that dresser. I'd been certain I wouldn't be at Kindle Home long enough for it to be worth my while. But I wanted to put my things in the drawers now, even if they would stay there for only another week or so.

"Lucy," Leon said. "I don't think you—"

I turned to him, tightly clutching a pair of my socks. "Leon, I do understand. And it's not that I *want* to go to Rabbit Island. I know how much you hated it there. It just feels different now. More bearable. Now that I know there's someone who gives a damn about me." Two people, I thought—Leon and Nate.

Leon stared at me. Finally, he shook his head and laughed. "Wait a minute. Remind me who's the counselor here, and who's the kid."

"Does it matter?"

"No," he said, and we stepped together for my second great hug of that day.

Just after midnight, Mrs. Morgan did the first of the night's spot checks. When she was gone, I made sure

Yolanda was asleep, then slipped out of bed and started for the attic. It was the third night in a row that I'd snuck out after hours, but I wasn't even a little tired. I was too excited. I was going to catch myself an arsonist.

I'd thought about the clues—the burned-out taillight, the footprints in the mud, Alicia's smug expression—but I still had no idea who it was. *Was* it Alicia, still trying to destroy Nate and me both for daring to defy her, and determined to strike a blow for spoiled rich girls everywhere? Or was it Joy, convinced that she'd have an easier time being Queen Bee at some other hive, and maybe still trying to get back at me for standing up to her? Or was it Emil, blinded by his hatred of all things group home, and driven by some mysterious inner demon of his own?

I didn't know who it was, but I knew they would strike again. Why was I so sure? Because the whole city now thought Nate Brandon was the one who had lit the fires. But if the point of the fires was to get Kindle Home shut down—and I was certain it was!—Nate Brandon was exactly the wrong person to be fingered for the crime. As long as everyone thought that Nate had set the fires, the pressure was off us Kindle Home kids. No, the arsonist needed to set another fire, soon, while Nate was still locked up in Ragman Hall, so the suspicion would be thrown back on us.

I reached the door to the attic and quickly stepped inside, softly closing it behind me. Then I crept up the darkened steps, just like I'd done twice before. I was tingling, I was so eager. I'd never felt so determined in my whole life. But catching the arsonist wasn't about not getting sent to Rabbit Island, or even about staying at Kindle Home. Those things didn't matter anymore. Neither did the Group Home Code. If it turned out to be Joy who was starting the fires, I'd happily turn her in, no matter what the consequences to me were. No, catching the arsonist now was all about Nate. He'd sacrificed everything for me by taking responsibility for a crime he hadn't committed. I needed to prove him innocent. And the only way I could do that was by using his camcorder to prove that someone else was setting those fires.

At the top of the steps, I started down the narrow pathway across the darkened attic, to the window on the other side. I took it slowly, but now it was as if I had some kind of ESP, and I knew where absolutely everything was. The floorboards didn't even creak under my feet.

I reached the window and opened it. Then I turned to the place where I'd hidden the rope, camcorder, and change of clothes. I picked up the rope and began tying it firmly around one of the attic's center beams.

Now the floorboards creaked.

I froze. The sound hadn't come from near me, but from the other side of the attic, on the opposite side of the stairwell. Was it the house settling?

The floorboards creaked again.

I wasn't alone. Someone was in that attic with me—I was sure of it!

Suddenly, I was drowning in the darkness. I clutched the coil of rope like it was a lifeline, but it offered no comfort. Then I heard a metallic *chink*, like a chain being pulled, like the sound of a bare light bulb being turned on.

Light flooded the attic. For a second, the flash blinded me. Then I blinked and finally saw the face of the person who had pulled the chain on the light bulb hanging from the ceiling.

It was Mrs. Morgan, and I don't think I'd ever seen anyone frowning so deeply in my whole entire life.

14

"Lucy," Mrs. Morgan said, glaring at me in the attic, in the harsh light of that bare bulb. She only spoke that one word, but it contained a whole dictionary's worth of disappointment.

"What are you—?" I had been starting to ask her what she had been doing there, in the dark, in the attic, in the middle of the night. But I knew. There was only one explanation. She had been waiting. She had probably planned to wait up here all night long, in between her spot checks. She had been trying to catch whoever was climbing out through the window in the middle of the night. It figured it was Mrs. Morgan, the strictest counselor in the house. Why couldn't it have been Leon?

I thought about lying, about saying that I had come up to the attic because I couldn't sleep. Or that I thought I'd heard someone up here, and that I'd come up to check it out. But there was no chance that Mrs. Morgan would believe me. I was standing by an open window with a coil of rope in my hands. If I tried to lie now, I knew I'd just piss her off more.

"How did you know?" I asked.

She breathed a heavy sigh. "Lucy, I know this house like it's my own. When the attic door was left unlocked, I knew someone had been up here." She stared at me, then shook her head. "So you're the one who's been setting the fires."

"No!" I spoke loudly, without remembering where I was. "No," I said, more quietly. "I was trying to *catch* the person setting the fires."

"Oh, Lucy." When she spoke my name, her voice dropped like a rock. My words weren't pissing Mrs. Morgan off—they were just disappointing her more. I almost wished she would get angry, like she had the day she'd found those pills in my bedroom. Anger I could react against. Disappointment just made me feel shitty. The funny thing was, I was actually telling the truth.

"Was that boy your boyfriend?" Mrs. Morgan asked.

"No," I said, and I felt my eyes shift. "Well, yes, but it's not the way it sounds. He wasn't guilty either.

We were *both* trying to catch the person setting the fires. I know I shouldn't have snuck out, but I was only trying to save Kindle Home. I figured if I could prove it wasn't someone from here, then they couldn't shut us down. And we *did* catch them—last night! We got the whole thing on Nate's camcorder. Only it was too dark to make out who it was. And then the car started burning, and we tried to put it out, and that's when the police caught us. Nate made me leave, and he took all the blame, which is why I was going out tonight—to prove that it wasn't Nate who had set the fires in the first place!"

The words came gushing out of me like water from a fire hydrant, and it was still all the truth. But as I was speaking, Mrs. Morgan lifted her hands to her face, rubbing her eyes like she was starting to cry. I kept thinking she couldn't possibly look any more disappointed in me, but then she did.

What was the point? I thought. There was no way she was going to believe me. It was too incredible. No adult would ever believe me. Probably not even Leon.

"Forget it," I said. I turned to the window, then closed and locked it. "Let's just go. I won't try to sneak out again, but you can sit outside my door if you want. And tomorrow morning, you can send me wherever you want."

Mrs. Morgan frowned at me some more as I untied the rope from the beam, then added it to the coil around my shoulder. Then I reached down to get the camcorder and my change of clothing.

I stood up again. "I'm ready."

Mrs. Morgan was still staring at me. But she didn't look disappointed anymore. Now she looked confused.

"What?" I said. Then I realized she wasn't staring at me, but at the object in my hand. Nate's camcorder.

"What is that?" she asked.

"Huh? Oh. Forget it. You won't believe me anyway."

"Lucy Pitt, what *is* that?"

It was comforting to hear her call me by my full name. Wasn't that how parents talked to their kids when they were angry? "It's Nate's camcorder," I said.

"Why do you have it?" Her eyes narrowed. "Did you steal it?"

"No. No! I told you, it's Nate's. We were trying to catch the person setting the car fires."

She kept staring at me. But the hesitation still hadn't left her eyes.

"Take a look," I said. "I told you we got the person on video last night. It's just too dark. You can't tell who it is."

I stepped over to her and showed her the tiny view screen. Then I played the file we'd made the night before. There was the darkened figure with the gas can, the quiet sound of the splashing. It even had the date and everything. After a second, you could also hear Nate's and my voices.

"We need to get closer," said the recording of my voice, just as the shadowy figure on the view screen lit a match.

From the little speaker on that camcorder, Nate and I both sucked in our breath.

"*No!*" I shouted in the recording.

On the view screen, the shadowy figure turned toward us. Then it whirled away. The screen was too small to see the flinging of the lit match, but I knew what would happen next.

Tiny flames leaped up in front of the car.

"No," said the recording of my voice.

"The gasoline!" Nate's voice said. "It must've dripped from the car!"

"We have to put it out before the car catches!" my voice said, and that's when the screen went dead. That's when I'd taken my finger off the button on the camcorder and it had stopped recording.

Mrs. Morgan didn't say a word.

Suddenly, she needed to sit. She turned for the nearby rocking chair and lowered herself into the seat. For the first time since I'd met her, she seemed very old.

"Why didn't you tell anyone this?" she said.

"Huh?" The question made no sense. Who would I tell?

"Lucy Pitt!"

"Well, I guess I thought no one would believe me."

Mrs. Morgan's eyes had lost all focus. "So it's true. You really *were* trying to catch the arsonist. You were trying to save Kindle Home."

I wasn't sure if these were questions or not, but I nodded anyway.

Her eyes latched on to me. "If I hadn't caught you here tonight, what would you have done?"

I had to think about that. Not because I didn't know, but because I wasn't sure what I wanted to tell her. Finally, I decided to just tell the truth.

"I would've gone out and tried to find the arsonist,"

I said. "If I had, I would've tried to get the whole thing on the camcorder."

"But if you'd been caught, the police would have thought you were setting more fires. The consequences for you would have been horrible. And even if you hadn't been caught and you *had* recorded the arsonist, how would you have explained the tape? You would have had to admit you snuck out of the house at night. The consequences for that would have been almost as bad." *Would have* been bad? I thought to myself. Did that mean I might not get punished for trying to sneak out—or for admitting to sneaking out twice before?

But all I could do was shrug. "I didn't care what happened to me," I said. "I had to help Nate."

Mrs. Morgan began to rock ever so slightly. It looked like she was nodding, but it may have just been the rolling of the chair. Underneath that rocker, the floor squeaked again.

"Do you know why I'm here?" she asked.

"Well, you knew that someone had been coming up into the attic—"

"No, not here in the attic. Here at Kindle Home."

"Oh. No."

"You children never wondered about my past?

About where I came from?"

I had to think again. Finally, I said, "No." I'd heard gossip about every other counselor at Kindle Home, just like I'd heard gossip about every counselor at every group home I'd ever lived in. But I didn't remember anyone ever saying anything about Mrs. Morgan, except that she'd lost her sense of smell. She was the kind of person who you thought would somehow *know* if you dared to gossip about her, the way dogs can sense fear.

"I had a husband and two children," Mrs. Morgan said as her eyes lost their focus again. "Seventeen years ago, they were killed in an automobile accident. The sense of loss was indescribable. The only way I could cope was by moving away. Eventually, I found myself here, and I've been working here ever since."

Why was she telling me such a personal story? Didn't she know I could use it against her? At the same time, I couldn't help but realize that Mrs. Morgan's story was a lot like mine. We'd both ended up at Kindle Home because our families had been killed in car crashes.

"So much despair," she muttered. "It's a wonder it all fits inside one single house."

I watched as Mrs. Morgan continued to rock slowly in her chair, nodding at me—or maybe not.

Finally, she looked up at me again. To my surprise, she didn't look old anymore. Suddenly, her eyes had never seemed so sharp.

"Go," she said.

"What?" I said. "To bed, you mean?"

She stood up and started for the stairs. "No, I mean out the window. I won't tell anyone I saw you here, and I won't report you missing from your bed. Stay out all night if you have to. Just go catch whoever is lighting those fires, and get it all on tape. If you do catch them, I'll go to the police with you, and I'll say we made the tapes together. That way, we can save your boyfriend and Kindle Home too."

"But—"

She reached the stairs and stopped. "Just don't get caught. Because if anyone catches you outside alone, you'll be sent to Rabbit Island, and I'll be fired." With that, she turned and started down.

"Mrs. Morgan!"

Just before her head disappeared into the darkness of the stairwell, she stopped and looked back at me.

"Why?" I whispered.

"Because I've already lost one family," she said. "I'm not about to lose one more."

The moment my feet touched the ground, I heard a faint rustle from the front yard. Could it be? Had I stumbled upon the arsonist so soon? I couldn't imagine who else would be lurking around in the bushes this late at night.

I crept closer. If it was the arsonist, I couldn't let myself be seen. It didn't do me any good to just *catch* the person I was looking for. I needed to get them on the camcorder starting a car fire. That meant I might have to follow them for a while.

At the corner of the house, I stopped and peered out into the front yard. It seemed even bigger than I remembered.

The rustle had sounded like it was coming from somewhere inside the long hedge that separated Kindle Home from the yard next door. The hedge was neatly trimmed on the neighbor's side—they had a yard service that came every week, even this late in the fall. But on the Kindle Home side, it was wild and unruly. So unruly that I couldn't tell if there was someone hiding inside or not.

I waited.

One minute.

Then one minute more.

Nothing happened. The hedge didn't make a sound. Had it just been the wind?

I couldn't wait there all night, so I stepped out into the front yard.

When I was almost to the sidewalk, the hedge rustled again, just to my side.

I was standing right out in the open, with no nearby bushes to duck behind. I didn't dare move for fear that I'd make noise and scare away whoever it was. So I stayed right where I was, frozen, not breathing, hoping that whoever was in that hedge hadn't spotted me yet.

Then some branches snapped and out leaped Oliver, the Kindle Home cat. He stared at me, his tail swiping the air. He had that cat expression that looks both completely innocent and absolutely guilty at exactly the same time.

I felt myself exhale. "Oliver," I whispered, "you had me scared."

The cat sat down on his haunches, twisted his head around, and began to groom his back. The night was so still that even Oliver's quiet licking seemed to echo down the street.

Stepping around the cat, I started for the sidewalk again. Once there, I stopped in the shadow of the hedge and listened.

The only sound in the whole neighborhood was the sound of Oliver's licking. I looked up and down the street. I figured there would be fewer police cars now that they had caught Nate, the person they thought was setting the car fires. But I was pretty sure there would be a police car or two around somewhere.

The sound of Oliver grooming himself echoed in the still night air. But suddenly, it seemed really loud. And it didn't even sound that much like licking. Yeah, it sounded wet, like a cat's tongue. And it was a lapping noise. But it was almost *too* wet. And it seemed to get louder the more I listened.

I looked back at the cat.

Oliver was gone. He had padded silently away.

I glanced around the yard. I didn't see the cat anywhere. But I could still hear the sound of his licking.

That's when I knew it wasn't licking.

It was the gurgle of gasoline being poured from a gas can!

I turned my head back and forth, trying to get a sense of where it was coming from. To the left? To the right?

No. Directly in front of me—one street over at least. The sound was being funneled through the side yards of two houses, right to me.

Gripping the camcorder in my hands, I barreled forward. When I reached the yard across the street, I bounded my way through the junipers and gravel and grass. I sprinted my way through the yard of the second house too.

Finally, I burst onto the sidewalk one street over from Kindle Home.

I listened again.

The gurgling had stopped!

I turned left, gazing down the street. It was well lit by a nearby streetlight, but I didn't see anyone. The street was deserted.

I swung right. It was darker in this direction, between streetlights. I didn't see anyone here either, but my night vision had been ruined by the blaze of the other streetlight.

I squinted, but I still didn't see anything in the shadows. Had I gone the wrong direction? Had the sound of the gasoline been echoing from somewhere else? Did I need to go yet another street over?

Then the silhouette of a person sharpened in the gloom. He or she was standing, facing away, on the sidewalk, next to a car parked not even fifty feet away. There was a gas can at the person's feet—it looked like the same gas can I'd seen the night before. And the figure was holding a tiny white square in its hands—a book of matches!

Whoever it was, they had just doused the car with gasoline and were about to set it on fire!

Had the person heard me? I started to move, to duck down behind the car parked closest to me, so I could lean out and record the whole thing on the camcorder. But even as I did, the figure turned and looked right at me.

It was Yolanda.

15

"Yolanda?" I said. I stood up again and was now facing the person with the gas can and matches. And I was confused. What in the world was *Yolanda* doing here? Why wasn't she back in our room, asleep? She wasn't wearing a jacket. She was dressed only in a T-shirt and sweatpants—what she usually wore to bed—plus sneakers without socks. Was she sleepwalking? But then how had she gotten out of the house?

Yolanda looked just as surprised to see me. "Lucy?"

Camcorder at my side, I hurried toward her. "Yolanda, what are you *doing* out here?" Whatever the reason, I needed to get her back inside Kindle Home before a police car came passing by.

"Lucy, stop."

I did stop, but not because she'd told me to. I'd

just finally caught on to what was happening.

Yolanda was the one who had been setting the car fires!

Yolanda was the one who had been setting the car fires? It wasn't possible!

Or was it? I thought back to the night of the first fire, four days earlier. I'd been awoken by the sound of sirens, but Yolanda hadn't been in her bed. She'd come into the bedroom a few seconds later, pretending to tell me all about the car fire, but maybe she'd just been returning from setting the fire in the first place. As for the two previous nights, Yolanda had been in her bed when I'd left the room, but who was to say she'd stayed there? Neither of those two fires had happened right away. Yolanda could have been awake when I left, then snuck out after me. I'd been pretty sure there was at least one other non-alarmed exit from the house somewhere—maybe down in the basement. And I hadn't immediately returned home after either of those two fires either, so she would have had plenty of time to return to Kindle Home before me. This would have explained the footprints I'd seen in the mud traveling from the backyard to the front yard and then back again.

Okay, I thought, so maybe it *was* possible that she

had set the fires. But why in the world would she *want* to?

"Yolanda!" I said. "What the hell's going on?"

She turned away, hunching her back. "Go home, Lucy. This is none of your business."

"Oh, it's not, huh?" I said. "They're going to close Kindle Home because of these fires! It sure as hell *is* my business!"

Yolanda ignored me. I saw her shoulders flexing. Then I heard a short hissing sound.

The strike of a match!

"Yolanda!" I said. I dropped the camcorder and started running toward her. "*Stop!*"

The match must not have lit, because Yolanda's shoulders flexed again.

I reached her at last, grabbing her from behind by the biceps. "Yolanda—!"

I had barely touched her when she whirled around on me. "*Get away from me!*" There was a snarl in her voice. She looked like a mother bear defending her cub. But that was no cub she was defending—it was a gas-soaked car. And she was trying to defend it with a book of matches.

I took a step back. I was afraid. This was definitely not the fragile, innocent girl I thought I knew. I had expected someone in Kindle Home to have a meltdown tonight, but I never expected it to be her. Then again, I knew she had behavioral problems—she wouldn't have been at Kindle Home seven months after the death of her parents if she didn't.

"Please, Yolanda," I said, trying to keep things calm. "Tell me what you're doing. Explain it to me."

She fumbled for another match from the little white book. "Go away!"

She struck the match, and it lit up. "Ha!"

As soon as it did, I reached out and snatched it from her hand. I felt it go out as my hand closed around the flame.

"*No!*" Yolanda shouted, and she lunged forward to grab the match back. We struggled, but I didn't let her take it back. As we fought, she kicked the gas can at her feet. The top was open, and gasoline spattered up onto her clothes.

"Give it back!" Yolanda said.

"It's out!" I said. "It's already burned out!"

Yolanda gave up at last, but I didn't let myself relax. For all I knew, that book in her other hand was full of fresh matches.

"Why?" I said. "Why do you want to do this? Kindle Home is the best place I've ever lived!

It's almost like a real home!"

The fury was back in her eyes, even stronger than before. "*It's not my home!*"

"What?" I said, confused again.

"It's *not*! Those aren't my parents!"

And suddenly, I remembered something I'd heard the first time I'd eavesdropped on the counselors in the office below the Magic Step. Leon had said that when an older kid loses a parent, that kid is sometimes afraid that bonding with any new adults would be "betraying" that lost parent. When he'd said this, I'd thought it was bullshit, at least when it came to me. But maybe it wasn't bullshit, not when it came to Yolanda.

Is this what Yolanda thought—that the Kindle Home counselors were somehow trying to replace her parents? And were these car fires her attempt to punish them for that, or just to stop them? But would Yolanda really want to screw a whole houseful of kids just to get back at some adults who weren't doing anything wrong to begin with? That seemed pretty warped, even by group home standards.

Unless it was all unconscious. Hadn't Leon said something about that too—that people didn't always know the real reasons why they did the things they did? It was like when I'd dogged Nate in the hallway. I hadn't known at first that I'd really been trying to push him away from me.

"Yolanda!" I said. "It's okay! Everything will be okay!" I remembered how Nate and Leon had both hugged me earlier in the day, and how good both those hugs had felt. So I reached out my arms for her.

She hissed at me, not like a person, not even like a wild animal anymore. She sounded almost like that match she'd lit, before I'd put it out with my hand. And suddenly, I saw Yolanda the way Emil saw me. She was out of her mind. I could see it in her eyes. She was a raging wildfire, ready to destroy anything and everything in her path.

Part of me was scared by that wild look in her eyes. But another part of me wasn't. That part of me recognized the look in Yolanda's eyes. In a way, those were my eyes, and looking at them was a little bit like looking into a mirror. I'd been where Yolanda was now—out of control, overcome by feelings I didn't understand. I must have been there when I'd attacked Nate in second-period biology, and those times when I'd almost had it out with Joy, and all the other fights I'd been in too. It wasn't just Alicia who was Fire. I was too. I was Ice *and* Fire. But there was another side to me and Yolanda, a side that Emil couldn't see. Yeah, we were fires, and sometimes we did burn out of control. But there is a beauty in fire—and a strength, and a passion. And I wasn't about to let Yolanda's fire destroy itself.

I stepped forward and wrapped my arms around her. Sometimes, the only way to stop a fire is with another fire—the controlled burn—and if I'd learned anything at Kindle Home, it was that I could control my burn. And if that didn't work, I'd freeze her with my icy resolve! No matter what, I was determined to stop her.

"Listen to me!" I said, hugging her tightly, holding her back. "It's okay! Everything's going to be all right!"

She immediately started struggling. She pushed and kicked and finally squirmed her way out of my arms.

"Yolanda, stop!"

She still didn't listen. Instead, she hunched down, wrestling with the little pack of matches again. She quickly tore one free.

"No!" I said. "Don't light that!"

It was too late. The match struck. It flared up.

And it kept on flaring. When she'd kicked the gas can, some of the gas had splashed on her clothes. Now it was lighting up too.

Yolanda yelped and dropped the match, but it was too late. Her sweatpants and T-shirt exploded into flames.

She screamed, even as she helplessly flailed her arms.

I didn't think, I just leaped forward, crashing into her, wrapping my arms around her, hugging her again. She was still screaming and burning, and I could feel the heat of the fire against my own clothes and skin, but I wrenched us both to the ground. Then, with my arms still wrapped around her, I started rolling back and forth on the pavement. I knew I was being burned now too, but I felt no pain. I just kept rolling, back and forth, back and forth, until we were like one person, one single fire. But I still didn't stop. I would roll forever until that fire went out.

The second it did, I heard loud voices all around me.

And that's when I must've passed out.

Epilogue

Whenever someone wakes up in a hospital in the movies, they always think they're in heaven. But when I woke up, I knew right away I was in a hospital. I doubt heaven smells like ammonia, and I bet the beds are softer too.

But there was one part of that hospital that seemed a lot like heaven. It was Nate, sitting in a chair next to my bed reading a copy of *Snowboarder* magazine. To my eyes, he looked better than any angel.

"Nate?" I said. My throat was sore, like I'd been shouting.

He looked at me, and his face lit up like a fluorescent light.

"You're awake!" he said. He rolled his chair closer to the bed so he was right next to me.

"Where am I? What happened?"

"You're in the hospital. You're fine. Especially now that you're awake."

"Yolanda," I said, remembering. "Where is she? Is she okay?" I started looking around the room, which was pretty stupid, since there was only one other bed, and it was obviously unoccupied.

Nate looked away. "She's okay. She's in the hospital too."

"Where?" I said. "Is she nearby? I need to see her."

"Not this hospital. A different one." He hesitated. "A different kind of hospital."

"What? Why?"

"It's a mental hospital. Yolanda has problems, Lucy. Six months ago, she tried to poison her foster family. Three months ago, at her last group home, she left the gas oven on."

So I'd been right. Yolanda was lashing out at anyone who tried to replace her beloved parents.

"Is she okay?" I said.

"She was burned more than you. But she's awake. She'll be okay."

It was only then that I realized there were stiff bandages on my body, on my chest and legs. There was pain too, big patches of it, like really bad carpet burns.

"You!" I said. "How'd you get out of Ragman Hall?" I couldn't believe that hadn't been the first question out of my mouth.

He smiled again. "They let me go. They had to when they learned that I wasn't the one who'd been setting the fires."

"But how did they—?"

"The neighbors."

"The neighbors?" I said.

"Don't you remember?"

I shook my head.

"When you were talking to Yolanda, trying to stop her from lighting the fire? There were people all around you."

"There were?" I hadn't noticed. I'd thought Yolanda and I were completely alone on that street. Then I remembered the voices right before I passed out.

"The neighbors heard you shouting and came out to see what was going on," Nate said. "So they saw and heard everything. Mrs. Morgan filled in the rest. And then there was the camcorder. That pretty much clinched it. You know, you're even kind of a hero. Article in the paper and everything. And I bet there'll be another one now that you're awake."

"Wait a minute. How long have I been here?"

"Three days. You weren't in a coma or anything, but they had you on painkillers."

"Three days?" That explained the tubes that were attached to my arm, and the little container of liquid hanging by my bed.

"You did it," Nate said. "You solved the mystery, you saved Yolanda's life, and you got me free. You should feel pretty proud."

"No," I said, but I guess I did feel a little proud.

"Thanks," he said, and he leaned forward to kiss me. His shoulder pressing against my chest hurt my burns, but I didn't say anything, because it was worth it to kiss him again.

Finally, we broke our kiss, and I said, "What about Kindle Home?"

Nate sat back in his chair. Suddenly, he wouldn't look me in the eye.

"What?" I said. "Tell me!" Nate wasn't touching my burns anymore, but I was a lot more uncomfortable now than when he'd had been leaning on my chest.

"Lucy, they're closing Kindle Home down. But not till the end of January."

"But you just said I'm a hero! There was an article about me in the paper!"

"I know. It completely sucks."

I sank back against my pillow. "So that's it. I'm still going to Rabbit Island anyway." Oh, well, I thought. I'd saved Yolanda's life, and I'd gotten Nate out of Ragman Hall. Those were the two most important things.

"No!" Nate said. "You're not going to Rabbit Island." He wasn't saying this like Leon had, like it was a vow or a promise. He was saying it like it was a fact.

"What?" I said, confused. "What are you talking about? Where am I going?"

"Leon wanted to be the one to tell you. He made me promise I'd wait." Nate grinned sheepishly. "But what the hell? I think you've waited long enough." And then he told me where I was going to live next.

I could hardly believe my ears.

I stared at the house in front of me. It was a lot smaller than Kindle Home. It was newer too, but definitely not new. The truth was, it was only slightly less of a dump than Kindle Home, and it didn't have any of the group home's interesting parts.

"This is it?" I said to Leon, who was standing right next to me.

"This is it," he said.

I didn't move, just kept staring at what would be my new home. A foster home. A foster home with Ben and Gina as my foster parents, and with Damon as the other foster kid. I wasn't supposed to know it, but Ben and Gina were even starting adoption proceedings on us both.

Unlike the house in *Heidi*, it wasn't a mountain cabin, and it probably didn't have a sleeping loft or a big stone fireplace. It definitely wasn't perched on a rocky cliff overlooking jagged, snow-covered peaks and fields of goats and wildflowers. But it was still perfect.

"Let's go inside," Leon said.

I wasn't ready to go inside yet. I'd been out of the hospital for a few weeks. And I'd had all that time to adjust to the idea of this new living arrangement. But part of me was still afraid that if I took a step toward the house, it would fade, and I'd see that it had all been just another daydream.

"It was you," I said to Leon. "You talked Ben and Gina into this."

He laughed. "If you think that, then you don't know Gina very well. I can't imagine talking her into anything."

"But why? Why would they do this?"

"Because they're tired of group homes. Always too many kids and never enough money. But they love kids, and they can't have any of their own. So they decided to get other jobs and do the foster-parent thing for a while. Left Mrs. Morgan and me to work the trenches alone and to keep fighting Emil."

"But how'd they get me out of The System? I mean, I'm a high-risk kid!"

He laughed again. "Are you kidding? It's the high-risk kids that The System is trying hardest to get rid of. Someone *volunteers* to foster you and they can't get the papers signed fast enough. Your little heroics with Yolanda didn't hurt either."

"I still think you had something to do with this," I said.

Leon coughed. "Well, I may have put in a good word here and there."

"Thanks," I said, and I couldn't believe I was starting to cry. Had I turned into a wimp or what? But I couldn't help it. Leon had promised me that I wouldn't end up at Eat-Their-Young Island, and I hadn't. But I'd never expected things to end up this good.

"Come on," he said, nodding toward the house.

"Let's go inside and wait for Ben and Gina."

Together, we walked up to the front door, and I grabbed the knob and tried to push it open.

It didn't budge.

"I don't believe it!" I said. "This door sticks too."

"No," Leon said. "It's locked. But Ben and Gina asked me to give you this." He dug into his pocket and held up a single gold key.

I was trembling when I took the key from his hand and slipped it into the lock. I heard it click open. Then I turned the knob, pushed the door again, and stepped inside.

ACKNOWLEDGMENTS

If a book is anything like a house, this one had a very strong foundation. The following groups and individuals have been essential in the construction of this book and of my entire writing career.

All thanks must begin with my partner since 1992, Michael Jensen. By deciding to spend his life with me, and by enthusiastically supporting my decision to be a writer of fiction, Michael has made countless sacrifices. A writer himself, he has also generously given me invaluable feedback on almost every aspect of this book. If we'd never met, this book would be less impressive than it is. For that matter, so would my life.

Much credit must also go to Jennifer DeChiara and everyone at the Jennifer DeChiara Literary Agency. In addition to being possibly the world's best literary agent, Jennifer is my mentor, my champion, my friend, and my mom (don't ask). I don't know how you thank a person for making your dreams come true, except to say, Thanks again, Jennifer.

So many of my writer friends complain about the shabby treatment they have received from their editors and publishers; I can't relate. I have only praise for the advice and support of my gifted and generous editor, Stephen Fraser. I suppose Steve must have some flaws, but if so, I haven't seen them. Everyone else at my publishing house, HarperCollins, has been absolutely terrific too, including Victoria Ingham, Margaret Miller, Molly Magill, Alison Donalty, Rob Hult, Janet Frick, Suzanne Daghlian, and Vanessa Amador.

If not for my friends' never-ending faith in me, I might have given up writing years ago. I am particularly indebted to Tom Baer, Tim Cathersal, Laura South-Oryshchyn, Danny Oryshchyn, Lynn Sauriol, and my parents, Harold and Mary Anne Hartinger. Plenty of other people provided emotional or professional support just when I needed it most, including Robin Fisher, Jay Gladstein, Nina Cathersal, Tina Smallbeck, Judy Blume, Dave Hanson, John McMurria, Linda Wood, Megan Matthew, Chris Jensen, Christy Wood, Michael Cart, Susan Schulman, Lisa Hake, Troy Johnson, Dennis Hensley, JoAnn Jett, Alex Sanchez, Peter Rubie, Brian Malloy, Lois Lowry; my godmother, Michelle Doran; my website collaborator, Greg Glick; and the Society of Children's Book Writers and Illustrators (SCBWI).

Finally, I want to acknowledge the former staff and residents of Bacon Home in Bellingham, Washington, where I worked over a decade ago and which has since been closed down. My stint as a group home counselor was short, but long enough for me to come to profoundly respect the dedication and the great sacrifices of the adults who make careers in foster care, and the amazing strength and courage of the kids they oversee.